KING OF THE HIGHBINDERS

KING OF THE HIGHBINDERS

Tim Champlin

Thorndike Press • **Chivers Press**
Thorndike, Maine USA **Bath, England**

This Large Print edition is published by Thorndike Press, USA and by Chivers Press, England.

Published in 1997 in the U.S. by arrangement with Golden West Literary Agency.

Published in 1997 in the U.K. by arrangement with the author.

U.S. Hardcover   0-7862-0898-8   (Western Series Edition)
U.K. Hardcover   0-7451-8800-1   (Chivers Large Print)
U.K. Softcover   0-7451-8801-X   (Camden Large Print)

Thorndike Large Print ® Western Series.

The text of this Large Print edition is unabridged.
Other aspects of the book may vary from the original edition.

Set in 16 pt. Bookman Old Style.

Printed in the United States on permanent paper.

British Library Cataloguing in Publication Data available

Library of Congress Cataloging in Publication Data

Champlin, Tim, 1937–
    King of the highbinders / Tim Champlin.
        p.   cm.
    ISBN 0-7862-0898-8 (lg. print : hc)
    1. Large type books.   I. Title.
    [PS3553.H265K56   1997]
    813'.54—dc20   96-36485

For my coworkers in
the Federal Service.

FOREWORD

Secret Chinese societies, later called tongs, have been known to exist in China for centuries. During that time they were organized for religious, fraternal, political, and criminal purposes. They were even set up for mutual protection during the early California Gold Rush days and later when thousands of Chinese came to build the Central Pacific Railroad.

What historians have labeled as the "Tong Wars" in San Francisco's Chinatown district lasted for about thirty years, from 1876 until most of the city was destroyed by the great earthquake and fire of 1906. These "wars" were battles by rival criminal tongs for control of the Chinese underworld that consisted mainly of prostitution, gambling, and opium. It was not unlike the violent competition of big-city mobs during the Prohibition era of the 1920s. In the

1880s, the tongs contained anywhere from fifty to fifteen hundred members each, the largest being the Chee Kong tong. In spite of their terrorist activities, the tongs affected such names (in English translation) as: Progressive Pure-Hearted Brotherhood, Society of Pure, Upright Spirits, Perfect Harmony of Heaven Society, Peace and Benevolence Society, Society of Sacred and Beautiful Light, The Society as Peaceful as the Placid Sea.

Chinatown in the mid-1880s consisted of a twelve-block area in the north-central part of the city that was inhabited by thirty thousand Chinese — a population so dense that often bunks had to be used in shifts around the clock. Unlike most other immigrant groups who came to settle, these Chinese came primarily to make enough money so they could return home and live in relative luxury with their families. For the average Chinese man, "making his fortune" might consist of clearing as little as five hundred dollars plus steamship passage. Thus, the vast majority of those in Chinatown at this time were male. They had no interest in politics, in learning English, or in becoming U.S.

citizens. The average Chinese man was for self and family, with little interest in community or patriotism. He wanted to become a "Gum San Hock" from the "Gum San Ta Fow," a returnee from the Big City in the Land of the Golden Hills.

Because they were not planning to stay, they did not bring their wives and children to dwell among the "fan kwei," the foreign devils. Consequently, about ninety percent of all Chinese women landing at the Embarcadero were slave girls destined to be sold into prostitution.

Before the ascendancy of the tongs, what were known as the Six Companies controlled most of the life in Chinatown. These were benevolent societies that were formed to admit members who were from the same region of China. Members paid dues of from five to ten dollars and had certain privileges, such as monetary help in time of need and a place to gather, socialize, and conduct business. Or, in case of death, the company sometimes took care of having one's body shipped back to China for burial.

The well-to-do Chinese merchants who headed these Six Companies met regularly to resolve disputes and plan for the betterment of the Chinese community as a whole. The heads of these companies also dealt with local, state, and federal government officials on matters concerning the Chinese community. The tongs, however, gradually supplanted the Six Companies as the most powerful ruling force.

Until about 1870, Chinese-American relations were good. Then things began to change for the worse. Economic conditions changed. The different customs, dress, and language of the Chinese, along with their refusal to mix with the white population; the existence of the infamous opium dens; the gambling and the so-called "singsong" girls; all of this, along with the increasing amount of violent crime in Chinatown, gave rise to a large anti-coolie sentiment. Irish laborers and others, resentful of cheap Chinese labor, began to oppress and bully them. In 1873 the Queue Ordinance was passed. Also known as the Pigtail Law and the Bobtail Law, it required that all prisoners in the county jail have their hair cut to no longer than one inch. And Chinese were arrested and jailed for such things as violation of the Cubic Air Ordinance (sleeping too many to a room), and peddling without a license (a law unknown in China). Their hair was shorn, and the loss of queues shamed them. This law, a judge ruled in 1879, was aimed at only one segment of the population, and it was revoked.

When the tongs began to battle each other for control of the criminal activities in Chinatown, the killings were always among the Chinese. The leaders of the tongs did not want to bring down the full wrath of the law on themselves by murdering any whites. The hired assassins of the tongs, because their favorite weapons were cleavers and long, heavy knives and hatchets, added the term "hatchet man" to the American language.

The term "highbinder" was a slang word applied to criminals of the eastern cities from the very early 1800s. The term was widely used by the police of Boston and New York and later borrowed by law officers of the West. Eventually, in the 1870s, "highbinder" came to be applied almost exclusively to the criminals of San Francisco's Chinatown.

Most whites knew very little about

what occurred in this community. Even the police were not well informed. When the rate of violent crime began to increase, the whites mistakenly blamed the Six Companies, whom they saw as a separate government in violation of the Constitution, instead of blaming the tongs that were beginning to rule by terror.

The decent Chinese people did not revolt. Conditioned by centuries of corrupt dictators, warlords, and officials in China, individuals did not try to change the system. They just bent with the wind and survived. They endured; they did not overcome. Hence Mark Twain, and other prominent whites, saw the Chinese coolie as passive, peaceable, and long-suffering. Even the term "coolie," which was an Anglo-Indian word from Bengali, meant "burden-bearer," and originally meant "bitter work."

In China, the Manchus had been in power since they invaded from the north to overthrow the Ming Dynasty in 1644. They would rule until 1912. During the reign of these oppressive overlords, the Chinese people mounted many rebellions, the most serious of which was the Taiping Rebellion that lasted from 1850 until 1864 and almost succeeded in toppling the Manchus from power. But this rebellion was finally put down with the loss of millions of Chinese lives.

This, then, was San Francisco's Chinatown of the 1880s: a crowded world seen by most outsiders as full of filth, dark alleys, and darker deeds. It was a world in which the Chinese took care of their own affairs — one way or another.

Tim Champlin
Nashville, Tennessee
August 1988

CHAPTER 1

Jay McGraw was depressed. The misty rain blew against his face as he slapped the reins over the backs of his team of Percheron draft horses. It had rained for eight straight days almost without letup, and he found himself longing for the brilliant sun of the Arizona Territory he had recently left. Granted, the rain had been mostly light, but the constant dark, low-hanging clouds, mingled with the sea fog, had combined to put a damper on his usually bright spirit.

He hunched down in his coat collar and pulled his hat brim down to shield his face against the chill, wet wind. Except for the nightlife, San Francisco in mid-April was not the most cheerful place he had ever been. But then it would be dreary, muddy, snowmelt time back home in western Iowa in the small town of Vail he had left more than two years before.

14

He rode alone, high on the seat of the low-wheeled beer wagon he drove, listening to the clopping of the iron-shod hooves and grinding of the stout, iron-banded wheels. In four parallel racks behind were cradled twenty-eight full kegs of beer. The middle two rows in the specially built wagon were nearly upright; the outer two rows were canted outboard at a forty-five-degree angle for weight balance and for ease of loading and unloading. The kegs had just been loaded from the big vats at Wieland's Brewery on Second Street. His boss had given him this late Friday afternoon delivery just when Jay was thinking of going home to his rooming house and cleaning up for a night out with some of his friends. But no, the Fountain Beer Garden must have an extra large order of steam beer and lager for the big crowd that was anticipated this weekend. The weather was expected to fair up, and everyone would be out in the spring sunshine.

Well, no use complaining, he thought. He had been lucky to land this job when coming to the city about two months before, even though he got only five days of work each week and his salary was not large. His German boss was not one to waste money. In fact he often sent Jay out alone to make deliveries instead of providing the customary second man to help manhandle the heavy kegs and hogsheads.

"Dere vill be someone dere to help you unload," the old man had assured him in his heavy dialect when Jay questioned him about this. Don't talk; just do the job, Jay had reminded himself. He had been down to his last few dollars and was beginning to panic when his newfound friend, Frederick Casey, a city policeman he had met at a dance, persuaded the old German at Wieland's Brewery, Carl Bauer, to put him to work as a deliveryman. In this late winter of 1882 the number of unskilled laborers in this city far outstripped the number of unskilled jobs, he had discovered.

"The financial panic of the seventies may be over in other parts of the country," Casey had told him over a beer one evening, "but it's still hanging on here. One of the big problems is that these coolies will work for practically nothing. It's a buyer's market. There's going to be more trouble over this. I expect I'll be called out for riot duty before much longer."

"Riot duty?" Jay had asked.

"The out-of-work hooligans will want to take out their frustrations on somebody. They've done it before. We had a really bad summer here in '77. Wound up calling out the state militia to restore order. And just like before, the Chinese coolies are a handy target. The unemployed whites blame the heathens for stealing their jobs."

"What do you think about it?"

The young, black-haired Irish policeman grew solemn. "I try not to take sides. My job is to keep order and enforce the law. I have to be neutral, but it's a helluva job sometimes because I can see right and wrong on both sides."

Jay had taken a liking to Casey immediately. Like Jay, he was in his mid-twenties, fun-loving and athletic, with a good sense of humor. He was a second-generation Irishman with very fair skin, blue eyes, and black hair and mustache — a very handsome man in a blue uniform, as numerous San Francisco girls would attest.

Jay himself was not as fair, had dark brown hair, was lean and muscular and wasn't half bad-looking, if he did say so himself. And except for an untimely injury he would have been playing professional baseball with the Cincinnati team. Fred had introduced him to several girls he knew, and Jay had been straining his meager budget taking a different girl to parties, plays, and dances at least four nights a week for the past month. Fred never seemed to have financial problems. But he had been on the police force for five years and also received a little extra pay as a member of the Chinatown Squad.

Jay swung the team onto Market Street, the main thoroughfare, and then had to check the horses quickly to avoid hitting a well-dressed pedestrian who darted out in front of him. He swore involuntarily under his breath. The man just smiled and tipped his hat.

Jay glared at him briefly and then spoke to the team. "Up, Dan! Up, Fultz! Go, boys!" The big horses lunged ahead, regaining their momentum.

Jay's thoughts drifted off again as he automatically guided the team through the traffic of carriages, wagons, and horse-drawn trollies. It had gotten so dark Jay half expected to see the gas street lamps burning. Oh well, once he got this load delivered he'd make good time back to the brewery and then could get back to his room. His date for the theater tonight was Michelle Oster, an auburn-haired beauty he had just recently met. They were to meet Fred Casey and his date at the California Theater on Bush Street at eight — *if* he could get there in time.

He saw the lights and the bulk of the magnificent Palace Hotel looming up a couple of blocks distant. With a deft pull of the reins he maneuvered the team and the heavy wagon around the corner off Market Street and started west.

"Hya! Giddap!" He popped the reins over the broad backs and the Percherons broke into a trot. The stoutly built wagon rumbled heavily over the wet paving stones without bouncing. The street was clear for the next block, and he had to make a run at the upcoming hill. He passed a loaded cable car and kept going, Dan and Fultz almost at a gallop. He eased them over to the right side of the street as they plunged up the hill. The team quickly slowed to a trot and then to a walk, feeling the drag of the heavy wagon behind them.

Jay whistled at the team. "Up, boys! Go!" He leaned forward on his seat and popped the reins, shouting them up to a greater effort. Muscles bunched under their sleek, wet coats as they threw their combined weights into the harness. Iron shoes clashed on the cobblestones.

Jay vaguely heard shouting some-where ahead of him, but he was concentrating so hard on his driving that he paid no attention to it. Some kind of political rally was always taking place.

The pitch grew steeper. "Up, Fultz! C'mon, Dan! Just a little farther, then we level off!"

The shouting grew louder, and Jay glanced to his right at a crowd of about three hundred men milling in a lot across from a hotel.

"Damn!" He looked again. It wasn't a crowd at a rally; it was an angry mob. About two-thirds of them were white men, most armed with pick handles and pistols. The rest were Chinese coolies, some in black hats and loose black jumpers and trousers. All the Chinese he could see wore the queue: the single, braided pigtail down the back.

The team had almost reached the in-tersection, where the street leveled off for a few yards before starting up the next block.

Just then the embattled coolies made a concerted rush to break out of the ring of encircling hoodlums. The shouting rose to a crescendo as the Chinese surged toward the street. Clubs rose and fell in the melee as the two groups merged and the hoodlums welcomed a chance to crack some Oriental heads.

A police whistle shrilled somewhere.

The mob surged over the sidewalk and spilled into the street just in front of the team, yelling. Two shots blasted very close. The horses jerked up short, tossing their heads and snorting. They jumped in unison and walled their eyes in panic as another shot exploded from the sidewalk only a few feet away. One of the Chinamen went down, grabbing at his leg. But Jay didn't have time to look anymore, as Dan and Fultz were beginning to rear and plunge. Attempting to escape the sudden noise, the horses were jerking to the left, their iron shoes slipping on the wet cobblestones.

"Whoa! Whoa, boys! Down, Dan! Down, Fultz!"

But Jay's shouts were almost lost in the screaming of the fighting mob that was now sweeping around the front of his wagon and bumping the near-side horse. Jay had his right foot jammed on the brake, but the iron wheel rims of the heavy wagon began to slide on the steep hill. The team was backing and dragging the wagon around to the left, in spite of the locked rear wheels. Jay anticipated they would go plunging back down the hill, away from the terrifying tumult, and he tried to guide them into a full U-turn but they were bumping each other. Jay suddenly felt the sliding rear wheel catch against something — maybe a trolley track. He didn't have time to look. The front wheels were cramped to the left. Wildly, Jay whipped the reins and yelled at the team to make them pull straight ahead, but it was too late. He felt the heavy load being over-balanced under him and the wagon began to tip.

"Oh no!"

It was going over and there was nothing he could do to stop it. At the last second he threw the reins and leapt off to the uphill side. It was a good six-foot drop, and he threw out both arms and tried to roll onto his shoulder as he hit the paving stones. But the landing nearly jarred the wind out of him.

Half-stunned, he rolled to a sitting position just in time to see wooden kegs of beer smashing onto the street as the wagon went over with a crash. The team was down, kicking and tangled in their harness. Other kegs rolled off and went bounding down the hill, and pedestrians ran for their lives. A young boy in knickers leapt up a light post just as a full barrel careened into the base of the post, spun, and then rolled away, still unbroken. A matronly woman in a floor-length dress saw one coming, screamed, and turned her back. The keg clipped her feet from under her and she sat down hard on her ample bustle.

The runaway kegs barreled into parked carriages, jumped the curbing, and smashed into storefronts.

The Clay Street cable car Jay had passed coming up, dummy car coupled to a trailer car, was loaded with well-dressed ladies and gentlemen. The gripman, seeing the accident, had released the cable and brought his cars to a stop about forty yards downhill. Just as Jay looked, two of the bounding kegs exploded against the front of the open car. Barrel staves flew in all directions. Gallons of golden lager were hurled into the air and descended on the passengers in a foaming shower. Women screamed. Sputtering, furious men jumped off the car, brushing rivulets off their sleeves. The feathers on several of the ladies' hats hung limply in their faces. Wailing and chattering rose from the assembly.

Two men had run to the team and were trying to unharness them. Fultz had managed to push up on his haunches, but Dan still lay kicking on his side, snarled under the double tree. Jay scrambled to his feet and ran to help get the team loose from the wagon.

Whistles were shrilling louder as the police came running to quell the riot. White hoodlums began to scatter as the uniformed men waded in, guns drawn and nightsticks flailing.

"Jay! What the hell are you doing here?" yelled a familiar voice.

Jay looked up from slashing a hopeless tangle of harness strap with his knife. It was Fred Casey.

Jay had to grin at the startled look on Casey's face. "Well, at least I didn't start it. What about you?"

"I was due to go off duty when all this busted loose and we got the call."

"Looks like the girls might have to wait awhile tonight," Jay observed, glancing around at the chaos in the street. The remaining coolies were fleeing as the blue-uniformed police got the hoodlums under control, handcuffing several and chasing others.

"I hope nobody got hurt with those kegs," Jay said, looking anxiously down the hill.

"See that group on the cable car?" said Fred Casey.

Jay nodded.

"I got a close look at them as I came up the hill. They're carrying a few placards with them. You'll never guess who just got a good soaking with Wieland's best."

"Who?"

"The Sons of Temperance."

CHAPTER 2

"Vee lost much money on zee accident yesterday. I haf been told dat you drove zee team right up to zee mob. And zay vere frightened by zee gunfire. Vun of our best teams, also. Lucky zay vere not injured badly."

Jay stood before the old man at Wieland's Brewery, trying to look apologetic. He knew he would be fired. There was no doubt about it. As he waited for the ax to fall he studied the old man's face. It seemed it was made up mostly of bushy white eyebrows and a huge white mustache that completely hid his mouth.

". . . feel dat you should be dismissed from your job . . ." the older man was saying. Ah, here it comes, Jay thought. Wonder what I'll do now? At least all they lost was the beer and most of the kegs, and part of a harness. The wagon had been only slightly damaged. No one on the street had been hurt. One store window had been broken. Maybe being fired was better than having to work for nothing to repay the loss to the company.

". . . but if anything should happen to dis delivery, you vill be finished here."

"What? I'm sorry," Jay stammered. "What was it you're saying?"

The old man took a deep breath and looked disgusted. "I say dat Mr. Vieland vants you to make a special delivery today to zee Cliff House. You know it?"

Jay nodded, still not understanding. "You mean, then, that I'm not fired?"

The old man's patience was wearing thin. "Not at zis time. But vatch vhat you do or you vill be!" He wagged a warning finger at Jay.

Jay's hopes rose. He was getting another chance! He found the keg — twenty of them — already loaded on the delivery wagon when he went downstairs from the office to the loading dock. Another team was standing patiently in harness, tails swishing away the flies. They were a matched team of four big sorrels, with a white blaze on each forehead and hooves blackened until they shone. All had small, decorative red plumes fastened to their headstalls. The wagon was even one of the newer ones in the fleet, bigger and heavier than the one that he had dumped. It had the company name painted in bold lettering on each side. It was also low-wheeled and sturdily built, with a heavy under-carriage. The brass trim shone.

"The Cliff House, huh?" the foreman at the loading dock remarked, handing Jay the receipt book. "That's a lot o' beer. Somebody must be havin' a mighty big, fancy party out there. The old man's sending out a fancy rig. Reckon he wants to make a good impression to keep their business."

Jay climbed into the driver's seat, re-leased the brake, took up the reins and the long, flexible buggy whip from its socket.

"Wish I was going with you," the fore-man said. "Beautiful drive out that way."

Indeed it was a beautiful day for a drive out along the coast, Jay reflected as he swung the team and wagon out onto Second Street. The gloomy weather had finally broken, and the mid-morning sun was burning away the dense sea fog that had blanketed the city. The air was crisp and clean and the breeze smelled of salt. Jay inhaled a deep breath of the fresh morning. He felt good in spite of the exhausting day he had spent yesterday, followed by the accident, and then finally capped off by a late night at the theater and supper with the lovely Michelle Oster, accompanied by Fred Casey and his girl. He was a little short on sleep, but the weather invigorated him and banished all thoughts of being tired as he rolled out of the city along the coast toward Cliff House.

Fred Casey would be on his usual beat in Chinatown today, but Jay had made arrangements to get together with him on Sunday afternoon to cross to Oakland on the ferry and do some horseback riding beyond the city. Fred also had talked of introducing him to some friends in Oakland.

The April breeze blowing in off the ocean was chilly, and he was glad for the light jacket he wore.

For a time he felt there was a drag on the wagon, that it wasn't rolling as easily as it should. And the horses seemed to be working harder than normal. On a slight upgrade they were straining. After about two miles their sleek coats were becoming lathered. When he stopped he would check to make sure the wheels were properly greased, he decided, although he had heard no squealing of friction anywhere. A team like this should be able to haul this load with no problem.

Eventually, just before noon, Cliff House loomed up in the distance, near the Golden Gate. The five-story building, spired and turreted, looked to be hanging precariously over the edge of the cliff, but in reality was built on a jutting promontory of rock. And just offshore from Cliff House were the well-known Seal Rocks, several seamed and weathered piles of rock thrusting up from the surface of the sea just offshore. Cliff House stood out by itself. Since there was nothing near it the building appeared even larger than it was, and could be spotted from a good distance away.

Jay was still a good half to three-quarters of a mile away when he noticed that something was wrong. He could just make out figures running out in front of the building. Were they drunk? Some wild party going on? Like everyone else, he had heard about its reputation. But it seemed rather early in the day for such goings-on, even for Cliff House. Maybe the revelry was still going on from the night before.

The breeze brought him faint snatches of shouting voices. Then he saw what the problem was — and he almost dropped the reins. A swirl of the onshore breeze showed him smoke, pouring gray-white and thick from one of the upper windows. The place was on fire!

Even as he looked two more upper windows burst out, and smoke billowed from within. Smoke was curling out from under the eaves as well.

He kept the horses at a steady trot in spite of his instinctive urge to whip them to a gallop. It would do no good to get there any sooner; it would just tire out the horses. And, it appeared from the start the fire had gotten, there would be no need for a beer delivery today. The horses would just have to haul it all the way back to town, unless they could somehow use it to help put out the fire. But he would be fired for sure, unless the beer was bought and paid for by someone at Cliff House first.

The cold onshore wind began to blow even harder, and he could see the surf breaking and foaming around Seal

Rocks. The wind was spreading the fire quickly. More windows exploded outward and showers of glass and smoke poured out.

By the time he had pulled the team to a stop at Cliff House, the lower floors seemed to be fully enveloped in flame. About thirty or forty people, most of whom appeared to be employees of the place, were milling around outside, making some feeble attempts to form a bucket brigade. But to no avail. The only water available was from the ocean at the base of the cliff, only three or four containers were available, and it was too far down to the water.

But no amount of water from buckets would stem this blaze. The smoke grew blacker and denser, and Jay had to move his team and wagon on down the road about forty yards to avoid the choking smoke. Most of the upper three floors were engulfed by now, and he could hear the flames roaring and feel the heat of the fire as the wind gusted off the ocean toward him. The smoke was blacker now and a huge column of it poured upward, staining the blue sky. People in the city would be seeing the column and wondering whether a steamer might have blown up offshore.

Somewhere in the distance he heard the wild clanging of a fire bell. Then, a minute later, he could make out the long hook and ladder wagon coming toward him down the road, one man driving the team, one steering the rear wheels, and at least a dozen hard-hatted firemen clinging to the long wagon.

Jay hoped everyone was out of the building. If not, there would be no rescue now. The entire upper part of the building was burning fiercely, fanned by the strong wind. Flames were licking and crackling from every window. Above the roar of the fire he could hear beams crashing and glass breaking inside the structure somewhere.

As the hook and ladder wagon finally wheeled to a stop and the fire fighters piled off, Jay wondered if there were any hydrants nearby, here so far from the city. He was on the point of wrapping the reins around the brake handle and climbing down to see if he could help, when a swirling gust of wind forced a cloud of choking black smoke down on all the spectators who were standing on the road. Jay held his breath and closed his eyes against the stinging smoke.

When he opened them again two Chinese men, dressed in what appeared to be silk pajamas, were standing near him — two of the servants he had seen earlier when he drove up. Jay started toward the firemen to offer his help.

But the two Chinese were quickly on either side of him, blocking his way. Startled, he started to say something to them but caught his breath when he felt two sharp points pressing against his rib cage, one from each side.

"What . . . ?"

They motioned with their heads that he was to move back to his wagon. The knives they held against him were shielded by the long, loose sleeves they wore. Jay stepped back, nervously eyeing the two Orientals. Their faces were grim. They wore black, straight-brimmed hats and long queues down their backs. He was so taken aback he couldn't think clearly. His first thought was that these were Cliff House guards who had been ordered to keep spectators back. He saw other carriages rolling up and stopping to view the spectacular conflagration.

"What is this? What are you doing?"

One man motioned for him to climb to

the driver's seat. They said nothing. He wasn't even sure they understood or spoke English. But there was no mistaking their intent. He climbed up to the driver's seat. With a chill of fear he realized that these men were not guards and this was not a joke, as they climbed up on either side of him. In an instant of panic he looked for help. He would leap off the wagon and run for a fireman. But everyone he saw was looking toward the burning building. And looking down at the two razor-sharp dagger points he saw within inches of him made his urge to run subside. Two quick thrusts and he would be mortally wounded before he hit the street.

The man on the right unwrapped the reins and handed them to him, then pointed over his shoulder at the road going south down the coast.

Jay pretended not to understand. The man jabbed the dagger a little harder against him, shook the reins with his free hand, and then emphatically pointed down the road. Jay took one last, desperate look around to see if he could catch someone's eye and maybe yell for help. But everyone was intent on the fire and the fire fighters running here and there.

With a sinking heart he took the reins, reached around the man sitting on his right, and released the brake.

"Up, back! Back!" He eased the team back a few steps until he had enough clearance to turn around. The whole time he was alert to any chance he might have to knock the two smaller men off either side and whip the horses to a run before they could recover and jump back on. But these men must have known what he was thinking or they were practised at abduction, because they sat so close to him on each side that he hardly had room to move his arms to drive. He could feel himself beginning to sweat. If anyone happened to look his way, all he would see was a beer wagon being driven by a white man with two Chinese assistants in silk brocade sitting on the seat with him. Certainly nothing to get alarmed about.

He swung the team around and started south down the coast road at a walk. The Oriental on his right, who seemed the more aggressive of the two, motioned for him to go at a faster pace. Again he pretended not to understand the sign language. The Chinese man had no patience with this. He snatched the long buggy whip out of its socket and lashed the rumps of the sorrels. They leapt ahead as one, and Jay had to hold them back to a trot.

"Put that damn whip down! I can drive this team!" He glared at the Oriental. He hoped the man understood English. He was rewarded for his outburst by a sharp pain in his left side as the other man jabbed him lightly with his dagger. Jay could feel the sting as he was cut, and the warm blood began trickling down inside his shirt. He caught his breath and looked at the man, but the slit eyes and impassive face never gave a hint as to what he might be feeling. In spite of the chill wind off the ocean Jay could feel his armpits sweating. He made up his mind to drive the team wherever they wanted, at whatever pace they wanted. He hadn't the foggiest idea what they were after. Was it the beer? Surely not. What possible use would they have for twenty barrels of lager? Were they stealing it to sell? If so, why hadn't they simply waited until he had abandoned the wagon to help at the fire and then just climbed aboard and driven off? Maybe they were afraid that if he noticed he would raise an alarm and someone would be after them immediately. But now it was kidnapping as well as theft. What would they do with him? Dump him off when they got back to town? Surely they wouldn't harm him, or maybe kill him? He thrust the possibility from his mind as sweat began to soak his shirt under his light jacket. His mind was in a whirl. If they were stealing the wagon and team, they wouldn't be very inconspicuous driving around the city in a wagon with WIELAND'S BREWERY painted on each side in large letters. Maybe they weren't going back into the city at all but would continue on down the coast somewhere.

But this idea was discarded when they motioned for him to turn left back into the city. They eventually made several more turns, and Jay's eyes were constantly searching for a way to get off the wagon. Maybe he could jump off on a steep downgrade, throwing the reins so his Chinese abductors would have a runaway on their hands. But they sat even closer to him, the points of their daggers, hidden in their loose garments, never leaving his sides. The pedestrians and the other vehicles on the streets might have been miles away for all the good they did him. They even passed a uniformed policeman walking his beat near Montgomery Street and Jay tried desperately to catch his eye, but the man looked the other way. Jay even tried attracting his attention by yelling at the horses and cracking his whip, but the cop had stopped to chat with a pretty young matron and her child in front of a store window and paid no attention to the passing beer wagon.

Finally, Jay followed his captor's pointed directions and swung the team up DuPont Street and headed directly into the heart of Chinatown.

CHAPTER 3

Jay was not familiar with Chinatown, but the silent one on his right guided and directed him on a twisting, turning course for several blocks, until the only thing he was sure of was which direction was which by the position of the early afternoon sun.

The two Chinese finally directed him to pull the team and wagon into an alley so narrow that Jay thought at first the wagon would scrape the brick walls on either side. But it passed with more than two feet to spare. In the middle of the block, with three-story buildings on either side, the man reached across and grabbed the reins, pulling the team to a stop. He set the brake, took the whip from Jay, said something to his partner in Chinese, and stepped down from the wagon. Just where the wagon had stopped was a break in the solid brick buildings where a small, almost hidden courtyard opened up. Suddenly, out of nowhere, the courtyard was filled with more than a dozen Chinese coolies who quickly surrounded the wagon and began to manhandle the heavy beer kegs off the back.

Before Jay could see where they were taking them, the Chinaman who still sat on his left side said something in Chinese, grabbed his arm and, jabbing directions with his dagger, indicated he was to climb down. He did as he was told.

Then, just as suddenly as they had appeared at Cliff House, his two captors in the silk brocade were gone, to be replaced by two bigger, stockier Chinese in plain dress who were not nearly as gentle. They grabbed him by each arm and half dragged, half carried him a few yards down the narrow alley and rapped at a recessed wooden door. It was immediately opened by a tall, thin Oriental wearing a long, loose garment and sporting a wispy, drooping mustache. His eyes were only slits in his yellow, emaciated face. Without a word the two burly ones hustled Jay past this man and into the dim room. Jay was temporarily blinded after the brilliant sun-

41

shine, but a strange, scorched smell smote his nostrils. Some small candles were burning in the windowless room, but his eyes had a chance to focus on what was taking place before he found himself on the other side of the room being shoved down a rickety wooden staircase. When he reached the bottom of the stairs he began to see more clearly, and what he saw made his stomach churn.

Lying around the small room, on bunks next to the walls, were about seven or eight figures. Reclining on their sides with knees drawn up, dressed in their loose clothing, barefoot, with shoes under the bunks, were more than a half-dozen opium smokers. About half of them were drawing at the stems of pipes about two feet long while the others were already in a drug-induced stupor, experiencing hallucinations on the far side of consciousness, their pipes lying beside them on the floor. A flat, circular bowl near the end of the long pipe contained only a small opening, into which the smokers who had just started were inserting a small bead of the pliable drug. This bead of opium was then lighted by means of a slim stick that was first held over a small, smoky lamp by each bed. Those two or three who did not have bunks lay on reed mats on the floor along the walls. Jay could hear the stewing and frying of the juices of the drug as the smokers sucked the smoke through the stems of the pipes.

As he paused for a few seconds to take in this scene, he noticed how deathly quiet it was except for the soft stirring or shifting of a body. The atmosphere was so thick from the smoke of the burning opium and the continuous smoking of the lamps as to make Jay's lungs cry out for air. There was no ventilation in the room, and after a minute or so he felt as if he were going to vomit, or faint.

The burly Chinaman who had brought him down here to this second subterranean level had left him standing in the middle of the room while he went over to a table on the far side of the room to confer with another Chinaman who seemed to be in charge. He was not smoking but was apparently collecting the money and dispensing the supplies.

Jay had no idea where he was being taken, but he had a sudden, overpowering urge to make a break for the stairs.

He was beginning to get claustrophobic. He had heard about these opium dens from Fred Casey and others since he had come to San Francisco. The girls he and Fred dated discussed these terrible dens of iniquity that were reported to exist in the Chinatown district. They were repelled, yet fascinated at the same time. Of course, the closest contact the girls had had with these dens had been articles in *Leslie's*, and lurid tales and woodcut illustrations in the *Police Gazette*. Fred Casey, as a special policeman in Chinatown, had actually witnessed these hidden illegal sin dens. The girls had pumped him for more of the graphic details, and he had held them spellbound describing what he had seen on some of his rounds. There were even some deliciously chilling tales circulating that some white women sometimes frequented the opium dens.

The stench was nauseating in the close air. He had to make a break for it while his mind was still clear. But just then his captor came back, took him by the arm, and led him toward a door in the far end of the room. Jay relaxed and tried to appear as passive as possible, to put the man off his guard. Jay saw no weapon on the China-man, but very likely a knife or gun was concealed under his loose black jumper. Armed or not, the man out-weighed Jay by at least thirty pounds. He had to be over two hundred.

The man opened the door and started down another short flight of stairs. There was a smaller room at the bottom at the third subterranean level. It was empty, windowless, and almost airless. Jay noted the dank air, and a sudden wave of panic swept over him. He knew he was going to make a break for it. There was no way he was going to stay here.

His captor grabbed him by the shoul-der and started to shove him down the last two wooden steps into the dank hole, but Jay pivoted and buried his fist in the man's belly with all the force he could muster. The Chinaman doubled over with a grunt, but he didn't go down. He let go of Jay and Jay was all over him, chopping a fist at the man's nose. But this man was like a block. He seemed impervious to blows. After his initial surprise he stood at the bottom of the stairs, blocking Jay's way and parrying the blows with his arms and shoulders, with an enigmatic smile on his face. Apparently, this man needed no weapons other than his body. When Jay had first hit him. in the stomach he had been off balance and had not gotten all his weight behind the blow, but he had almost skinned his knuckles. The man was wearing some kind of flexible protective armor under his loose jumper.

When Jay finally stopped swinging and stood, panting, in front of him, the round, slant-eyed face widened still further in a silent smile. The only light in the tiny room was filtering down the stairs from the upper room. The Chinaman turned and started back up. But Jay resolved that he wasn't going to be left in the pitch blackness of this airless hole three floors below the street.

"Hey, you!" Jay shrieked.

The Chinaman turned back on the bottom step just in time to catch the toe of Jay's boot in his groin. There was no hidden armor there and he collapsed to his knees, gasping and grabbing at himself. Jay leapt over him and up the rickety wooden steps three at a time. But just as he burst through the door he saw something blur in front of him and felt a stunning blow at the base of his throat. Stars exploded before his eyes and he fell forward. Then a crushing blow landed on the back of his neck, and he felt as if he were falling into a black hole.

When Jay opened his eyes as consciousness returned, he experienced a moment of sudden panic in which he thought he had gone blind. Then he realized he was lying on his stomach in a totally dark room. His next sensation was one of pain. His neck, front and back, felt as if it were about to break off. As his hand went up to massage the tender muscles and to gingerly feel his windpipe, he recalled the pain of the previous blows. If they had not been delivered by an expert he could have been killed. Or maybe it was just blind luck. His head was throbbing from the rabbit punch. He rested his forehead, then his cheek, back down on the cool, packed floor. Or was it smooth slabs of rock, scattered with dirt? He couldn't tell which. All he knew was that his head didn't hurt as bad lying still as it did moving.

After a few minutes he pushed himself

up to a sitting position and waited for the throbbing to subside before carefully rotating his head and again feeling his neck. No permanent damage, he decided. But then he smelled the dank, stale air and knew another moment of panic. He was trapped in some sort of cave with no air or light. He would suffocate in a very short time. He had always had a touch of claustrophobia. Tight, close places had always made him nervous. He would invariably feel an instinctive panic rising from within him and begin looking for a quick way out. Dark, stuffy places were even worse. He was never able to go explore caves when the other kids would ignore their parent's warnings and head for those dangerous holes in the hillsides or riverbanks. He never understood how miners could work hundreds or thousands of feet below the earth's surface in hot tunnels that often contained dangerous gases.

He forced down the moment of panic and concentrated on thinking a way out of his present dilemma. First of all he needed to get an idea of where he was, since he still literally could not see his hand before his face. If this was a cave rather than a room, he had to be careful he didn't walk off some ledge in the dark. So he dropped to all fours and cautiously crawled straight ahead, feeling along the floor. His heart jumped into his throat and his pulse began to pound in his head as he heard a scurrying noise.

After a few seconds he started again, hoping his exploring hands wouldn't come into contact with a rat. To avoid this he stood up and slid his feet along the floor with hands extended in front of him. After about ten feet, his probing fingers found a wall. It was of some sort of masonry and stone, cracked and seamed. He wished he had some matches so he could at least see where he was. But not being a smoker he rarely carried matches. He felt his way along the wall, estimating its length. When he had done this for two walls, he discovered they were about ten or twelve feet each. On the third wall he tripped over the base of some wooden steps. By this time he was almost sure this was the same room he had tried to escape from. Apparently, he had been knocked unconscious and thrown back down into the same room.

He felt his way up the steps until he encountered the door at the top. There was no latch or handle on this side of it. It fit so tightly that no light leaked through around the edges; either that, or it was just as dark on the other side. Maybe the opium den he had seen was closed. He didn't know what time it was or how long he had been out. There was no possibility of forcing this door without some tools, as it was coated with some sort of smooth metal. He gave the door a tentative shove with his shoulder. It was like pushing against the stone wall. He came back down and felt his way around the rest of the room. If this was the room he had glimpsed earlier, it was perfectly bare of furniture or windows. He came back around to the steps again, feeling more and more like a blind man. The pupils of his eyes had to be very wide by now but they were collecting no light at all, just the velvety blackness everywhere. He made as much noise as possible, scuffling his feet and coughing to scare off any vermin that shared this black hole with him. He sat down dejectedly on the bottom step and leaned his elbows on his knees. As he remembered it the ceiling of the room was no more than seven feet high. The air was close and stale. If the room was indeed airtight, as it appeared to be, how much air did it contain? How long would it last? He held his hands against his temples to stop the throbbing. Was it from the blows or from the lack of oxygen? It had to be the blows. He didn't think he had been out long enough to have used up much of the air. He was sweating, and he stripped off the light jacket he still wore. Then he lay facedown on the floor and put his cheek against the cooler stone.

He lay there with thoughts whirling through his brain. What did these people want with him? If they wanted to kill him, they could have done it immediately. Torture? His mind recoiled at the thought. Ransom? He was not wealthy, and had no connections. Who would pay ransom for him? Surely Fred Casey could not. He was practically the only one he really knew in town, other than his employer. Wieland's Brewery could afford ransom. But why? It made no sense. If that were the motive, why not kidnap Lloyd Tevis, the head of Wells Fargo, or one of the bonanza silver kings like James Flood. Or even Senator Sharon, who resided in the city at least part of the time.

Finally he began to get drowsy. But he didn't want to fall asleep on this floor. Rats — or whatever he had heard rustling in the dark — could bite him. A chill went up his back at the thought. He forced himself to get up and feel his way back to the stairs, where he sat on the third step and lay back on the others. Higher up, the air was very bad and getting worse. He could tell the oxygen was being used up. He pondered the situation. Were they ever going to come and let him out of here? If not, he would cling to life as long as he possibly could. He became disoriented and began to tremble with a terrible fear — fear of death, fear of the unknown. But gradually he grew calmer and got himself under control. He scooted back down and lay facedown on the floor again, where the air at least seemed a little fresher. To hell with the rats or snakes or whatever else was in here with him. But try as he might to stay awake he began to get groggier. And then he knew nothing.

CHAPTER 4

He didn't know how long he slept, but it seemed like hours. He awoke, feeling drugged, when he found himself being dragged up off the floor. He gulped the air that was flooding in from somewhere. He got his wobbly legs under him and squinted at the light that was coming in from the open door at the head of the stairs. The light was dim, but after the total blackness he had experienced it was as welcome as the miracle of light to a blind man. Two Chinese men had him, one under each arm, and they half dragged him sideways up the steps. As his senses began to clear Jay wondered where he was being taken. But he really didn't care at this moment. Any place was better than this.

When they reached the opium den on the level above it was just as before, only more crowded. Jay wondered if it were day or night outside. Oh, to see the sky and smell the fresh air again! The den stank of the burning drug.

They paused in the middle of the crowded room and his two escorts pulled a cloth sack over his head. Then they pinned his arms behind him with a viselike, wiry grip — demonstrating a strength he wouldn't have thought they possessed, judging from their small stature.

Then he felt himself being walked through a door, up another flight. This should be the street level, Jay thought, trying to remember the details of where he was going. Then he was walked through several more doors connected by hallways of a sort. Some of the doors had to be unlocked as they paused, and he could hear metal clicking and bolts sliding. At one point they must have passed outside between two buildings, because he felt a rush of chill air and, for a few seconds, heard the clopping of a horse's hooves not far away. He also smelled putrefying garbage.

Feeling a sudden surge of desperation, he twisted his arms loose and broke away. But before he could even rip the sack off his head a blow to his midsection sent him doubling to the pavement, diaphragm temporarily paralyzed. He was yanked roughly to his feet still gasping to get his breath back. The pain didn't begin to subside until he had been hustled through another door and they were halfway up a steep flight of stairs. This time he resolved to go where they led without further resistance. He would figure out some way of escape later — although he had been totally unsuccessful at finding a way out of his airless prison.

Finally they stopped, and from somewhere in another room he heard the shimmering crash of a huge gong. As the echoes died away he heard the door before him open, and he was escorted forward. His feet encountered a soft carpet, and even through the cotton of the sack his nose picked up the odor of incense. He heard a sliding noise and a thud behind him as the door closed.

Someone yanked the sack off his head, and at the same time his arms were released. He stood there, blinking at the scene before him and rubbing the circulation back into his numb wrists. But the sight before him made him forget his own discomfort. At the far end of the room, a good sixty feet away, sat one of the biggest, strangest-looking men he had ever seen. For a moment or two Jay thought he was looking at a life-size wax figure of the Buddha. But then the figure moved and he knew the apparition was alive. Seated in an overstuffed chair on a raised platform was a huge mountain of a man, round skull completely bald, massive shoulders and arms. But as big as his head and shoulders were they appeared small when compared with the gigantic hemisphere of a belly they were perched above. He wore a white silk robe with loose sleeves which hung open in front. Worked into the silk on each side of the open robe were magnificent green and gold fire-breathing dragons. A matching pair of green silk drawers encased his legs, and on his feet were green and white slippers. This mountainous mound of flesh was half sitting, half reclining on a padded chair that more resembled a throne, with gold dragon heads worked into the top behind his head and the front of each arm. A gold chain with some sort of pendant Jay couldn't see was suspended from his neck, or where the neck would have been on a normal human. This creature's head rested directly on the trunk of his body. And Jay noted, as the man raised his hand to motion him forward, that he wore rings of what appeared to be gold and jade on several of his fingers.

Jay started forward numbly, trying to take in as much of the room as possible without turning his head. He walked on a runner of carpet that was bottle-green trimmed with gold. Fresh flowers decorated alabaster stands on each side of the throne. And four large braziers were burning, giving the room its light and also perfuming the air with some sort of delightful-smelling incense. Although the atmosphere was a little close with the cloying odor, it was not really unpleasant. On each side of the throne, standing as still as if they had been statues, were two burly Chinese Jay took to be bodyguards. They were dressed in loose green silk and each sported a queue. As the creature on the throne turned his head slightly, Jay noticed that he too had a thickly braided queue growing from the back of a head that was otherwise as hairless as a billiard ball.

Jay stopped a few feet from the Buddha-like figure and waited, his mind in a whirl. He was trying to keep his mental balance, but this whole strange experience had been so disorienting that he felt as if he had been whisked, by some magic, from his humdrum job in San Francisco to Canton. This outdid anything in his wildest dreams. And thinking of wild dreams, perhaps that's just what this is, Jay reflected. The creature's booming voice interrupted his thoughts.

"You lowly Caucasian scum! You do not even bow before the emperor of all China? You dog! Down on your knees!" he roared.

Before he could respond, one of the bodyguards sprang forward and literally kicked his feet from under him in one quick movement. Then the man forced Jay's head down so that his forehead touched the green carpet.

"Ah, that is more like it. Now, again, on your own."

Jay rose to his feet and then went down on his knees and touched his forehead to the floor.

"Now you may stand."

Jay rose.

The bodyguard had resumed his position to one side.

The round-headed one regarded Jay

for a few moments in silence.

"You don't appear to be as strong and daring as I was told," he began in perfect English with no trace of an accent. And yet he looked to be pure Chinese by race.

Jay said nothing. He tried to look humble and inconspicuous. Maybe despite whatever they wanted him for they would give up and let him go, in disgust at his dirty, unshaven appearance and his weak demeanor.

"But no matter. Looks can be very deceiving. You will do as we direct you or you will be disposed of and we will find someone else. However, at this point we have gone to considerable pains to select you and to set up our scheme. I am going to explain to you what this plan is, so you will know exactly what we expect from you." He paused and signaled his bodyguards, who took up large, long-handled fans and began fanning the imperious one.

"You have not been outside in the city for the past few hours, so you do not know what the latest sensation is in your white man's world. Well, I'll tell you. If you were out on the street at this moment, you would very likely be reading in the newspapers or discussing

59

with your friends today's headline in the *Chronicle*. This headline gives the terrible news that your own mint here in San Francisco has been lightened of a considerable number of gold coins: three million dollars worth of double eagles — freshly minted — to be exact."

The import of this incredible statement barely penetrated Jay's mind. He dismissed it as more of the ravings of a lunatic. Any man who would call himself the emperor of China would likely say most anything.

"Ah, you show no surprise at this?" The fat one seemed disappointed that his momentous statement had fallen on deaf ears.

"You doubt the power of Yen Ching, then, you offspring of a dog?" The round face went from placid to cruel, the slanted eyes mere slits in his face, his grim slash of a mouth turned down at the corners.

"Show him!" he shouted. "Show this mangy cur what power is ours!"

His two bodyguards were gone in a flash. They disappeared through a door behind the throne. Jay took advantage of the opportunity to glance around the room behind him to see if his two captors who had brought him here were still around. The room was empty except for himself and the huge man in front of him.

"There is no way out, if you are thinking of escape," the monster said. "The doors are locked and my guards are just outside. It would be foolish to think of attempting to escape."

Jay turned back to the front and did not answer the faint smile that was playing about the mouth in the huge head that lolled back against the padded throne.

Just then the door opened behind the throne and the two bodyguards reappeared, trundling something on a two-wheeled cart.

"Show him! Show him!" the big one cried like some spoiled child, gesturing impatiently.

Jay recognized one of the beer barrels that had been on his wagon when he was captured. WIELAND'S BREWERY was burned around the middle of it.

One of the men took a crowbar and pried up the top. Then the two of them turned the keg over in front of him. Instead of beer a flood of gold coins spilled out onto the green carpet with a dull, clinking noise. Several of the coins rolled out across the bare, wooden floor, finally rolling to a stop singly, with a ringing noise that echoed loudly in the big, bare room.

Jay could hardly believe his eyes. Yes, this had to be some sort of dream. He would wake up shortly and wonder at the seeming reality of it. He would tell Fred about it and his friend would remark again what a vivid imagination Jay had. Or he might tell him to quit eating fresh oysters just before going to bed. But even as he thought this he knew it was no dream, but some cruel, incomprehensible reality.

"There! There! You see?" shouted Yen Ching. "Go ahead, pick them up. Run your fingers through them. Look at the date and the mint mark."

Jay did as he was bidden. The coins were still wet. It appeared they had been rinsed with water, but some were still sticky with beer. He held several of the twenty-dollar gold pieces to the flickering light of the burning braziers. They glinted dully. They were all alike: the head of Liberty on the obverse and the eagle on the reverse, the milled edges. He could see at a glance that they were new and uncirculated. They all bore the date of the current year, 1882, with *s* at the bottom edge on the reverse.

He was amazed, but he feigned disinterest as he dropped them back onto the small pile in front of him.

"You have nothing to say?" cried the big man. He gestured at his two guards and said something in Chinese. They hurriedly began gathering up the gold hoard and putting the coins back into the small keg.

He did not speak again until the coins had been retrieved and the keg wheeled back through the door to the next room or vault or whatever was behind the throne.

"What you saw is only a small sample of what your government has so kindly and unwittingly donated to our cause." The creature almost smiled at his own humor.

Jay stood expressionless, hands at his sides, wondering where all of this was leading. The two bodyguards returned to stand in their former places, unobtrusively, on either side of the padded throne.

The monster shifted his bulk and attempted to sit up a little straighter in the chair. "You may be wondering just what all this has to do with you," he continued in his even voice. Jay had never seen anyone whose manner could change so suddenly from shouting rage to smiling, to petulance, to a businesslike tone. The man had to be a lunatic. But then if I were imprisoned in such a body maybe I would act the same way, Jay thought.

"The quality of patience which the Oriental possesses is something the world has known of for centuries," he went on. "Our people have learned patience the hard way, suffering from prehistoric days under tyrants and warlords and invaders. We have had much practice at learning the quality of patience."

Jay wished he would get to the point, but he realized that this man was enjoying his recitation. He would make the most of his posturing before his captive audience.

"The Manchus are only the latest in a long line of malevolent overlords. They swept down from the north and overran our people and the Ming Dynasty in 1644 and have been the ruling power in China ever since. These barbarian invaders from the north forced our people, as a sign of their servitude, to grow a long braided pigtail from the back of the head." He turned his head slightly and grasped his own queue. "Most of our people did not ride horses, so the queue became a practical way for a Manchu on horseback to seize a peasant. The queue became a sign of our shame."

He speaks as if he had been there, Jay thought.

"But our people endured this ignominy. In time we turned the queue into a sign of pride and defiance. The queue has become a symbol of Chinese patience and endurance. We may have reversed the original meaning of the queue, but the descendents of our Manchu conquerors still rule in China. Their power has been somewhat weakened by the heroic efforts of our people to overthrow them during what your leaders have chosen to call the Taiping Rebellion that ended only eighteen years ago with the brutal murder of millions of our valiant countrymen. The British and American governments gave much help to the brutal Manchus during the fourteen-year war. And for that they shall pay! In fact they have begun to pay already, in a very practical way." He attempted a smile again at his reference to the gold. "Yes, they will pay for another strike at the head of the snake that still sits on the throne of China. We will strike them while they are still weakened from long years of war. Many of those who are eager to rule their own country again are here in California, in the cities and in the mining camps. We are all gathering our strength, our money, and our manpower, both here and in China, to strike a killing blow at the tottering monster whose hoary head still trembles above millions of our countrymen."

The longer he talked the faster and louder he became, until Jay could see the flecks of spittle forming at the corners of his mouth. He was working himself into a good rage with his rantings about the Manchus.

He paused and signaled both of his bodyguards, who began fanning him again from either side with the wide, long-handled fans. Jay noted it had become rather stuffy in the big room with no windows and the burning incense, even though it was nothing like the room where he had been imprisoned. With a shudder he uttered a silent prayer that they would not return him to that dungeon.

Yen Ching seemed to gather himself, and dropped the subject of the Manchus for the moment.

"Not only are the Chinese patient, they have also endured and survived for centuries by learning to adapt and absorb many of the customs of their conquerors and turn them to their own advantage. For one thing, you hear that I speak perfect English. I daresay that very few whites in this city or this country speak Chinese in any of its dialects as well as I speak your language. I learned it in Hong Kong."

Jay had thought he detected a slight trace of British pronunciation in his speech.

"This ability to speak your language I have turned to my advantage. I despise most of your customs, but I will take what I need and leave the rest.

"My ability to speak English, along with my understanding of the greed of most white men, has enabled me to make contact with several of your underpaid civil servants, who are in positions where they can do me much good. Bribery of officials has been perfected to an art form in China over many years. It was not at all difficult to bribe some of your men to give me all the information I needed concerning the operation of your mint here, how and when and where the newly minted gold was shipped from the mint to other banks in other parts of the country. In fact I would say that your assayer was most cooperative, for the right amount of money, in giving us all the information we needed. Then it was a matter of plucking the flower just as it opened."

He smiled that strange smile again at the look of incredulity on Jay's face.

"But as you Caucasians are fond of saying, I must come to the point. We have the money — approximately three million dollars worth of twenty-dollar gold pieces — which we plan to use to further our cause of overthrowing the Manchu government in China. If you cooperate with us, you may someday tell your grandchildren that you actually stood in the presence of the Divine Emperor of China, for you are now looking at he who is to occupy the throne of our Celestial Empire. I have been brought up to the Third Heaven, and God Himself has revealed this to me."

The only heaven he has experienced is one induced by opium, Jay thought, trying to keep a poker face so this lunatic would not fly into a rage merely by misinterpreting the look on Jay's face.

"But I must use the resources at hand. One must have power to rule, just as the Chinese District is being ruled now by warring tongs. Unfortunately, they are fighting over petty criminal activities such as prostitution, opium, and fan-tan parlors, with no higher sense of purpose. But one must take things as he finds them, and thus I have made myself, as a first step toward glory, head of the most powerful tong in Chinatown, the Chee Kong tong. There are others who would unseat me and who, through envy, even seek my death. But they are as flies around the emperor's table. No force of hoodlums will unseat me. It has been destined from on high that I will overthrow the Manchus and rule the homeland of China, establishing a benevolent dynasty even greater than that of the Ming period. All of the other tongs will know shortly that it was I who engineered the taking of the gold from your mint. Then they will respect my power and maybe even come over to join me in the great plan."

Jay had previously had these tongs explained to him by Fred Casey, since Fred had some contact with their members nearly every day while on his beat in Chinatown. And this man claimed to be the head of the most powerful tong of them all. With a sinking feeling Jay realized that there was not much chance they were going to let him go, now that he knew that they were responsible for the robbery. His stomach was churning, but he tried to look properly humble by keeping his eyes downcast in the great presence.

"Ah, but I digress. You wish to know what your part is in all this. You are white. You have recently come here from the southern part of the Arizona Territory. Now that we have the gold, we must find a safer place from which to organize our revolution. I have decided that Mexico is that place. The government of Mexico is not as suspicious of foreigners. Their petty officials are also not as averse to taking bribes. But to get to Mexico from here overland will require a white man as guide who will not draw suspicion to our wagonloads of gold coins, disguised as trade goods. That's where you will help. You will be that guide. You are familiar with the country through which we must travel and with the people. You are one of them. You handle horses and mules well, you have no family here who will miss you if you disappear."

Jay had the urge to ask what his fate would be at the end of all this, but held his tongue.

"We will travel slowly, and avoid towns and settlements whenever possible. And we will travel at night as much as possible through the hot desert country. But I will leave those details up to you. When you succeed in leading us across the border, you will be free to go. And in addition to your life, you will be amply rewarded in gold. Should you try to run or betray us, you will be instantly killed."

"What is to prevent me from leading you to Mexico and then coming back to tell the authorities here where you are?" Jay finally dared ask, breaking a long silence.

"Once we have crossed the border we have a hiding place already prepared, and the Mexican government will not be able to find us. We have made very thorough advance plans. That is why you are here. I even had our Chinese servants set fire to Cliff House as a diversion so we could take you and your wagon. If you should go to the authorities with such a fantastic story of leading a small group of Chinese across Arizona to Mexico with a wagonload of stolen gold, and no one is able to find any trace of us, who will believe you? The gold that you will receive in payment will be untraceable.

"Now you will be taken to an apartment and made comfortable. It will be a few days before we are ready to depart. We must wait until the furor over the robbery begins to subside."

"My friends will come looking for me," Jay said calmly.

"You will not be found here by anyone." Yen Ching clapped his hands sharply.

Jay heard the door sliding open behind him, but he didn't even turn around as his two captors came up and placed the cloth sack over his head once more, then led him away.

As near as he could tell, they did not return the same way they had come. He thought they went into another building and eventually wound up at or near ground level. When they finally released him and removed the sack, he found himself in a rather small room that resembled that of a hotel, though furnished in a somewhat Oriental style. There was a pallet on the polished wooden floor, with cushions scattered here and there. A low wooden table inlaid with porcelain and mother-of-pearl was in the center of the room. But what drew his eyes immediately was one heavily barred window through which streamed daylight. However, it was situated about six feet off the floor in the middle of one brick wall. Without a word the two left him, bolting the door from the outside.

The fat one had been as good as his word. The room looked very comfortable. It was light and airy. Jay used the slop jar in the corner before he did anything else. Then he went around examining the room. The bottom of the window was an inch or two above his head. He dragged the low table over to the wall and stood on it, grasping the bars to look out. There was no glass in the window and he welcomed the smell of the cool air, even though it was slightly tainted with the smell of a cesspool somewhere and also the odor of food cooking. The window looked out onto an alleyway. He could not see the street in either direction. He was on the ground level and could see mostly the tops of the heads of a few Chinese figures moving up and down the alley. As near as he could tell from the light, he guessed it to be early morning.

"Help!" he yelled at the top of his voice. "Help! I'm being held prisoner here! Somebody help me!"

Two Chinese girls who were passing by looked up at him, said something to each other, giggled and kept going. A man glanced up curiously but kept walking without a word. Maybe they don't understand English, Jay thought. He tried yelling a few more times, but to no avail. Those few early pedestrians within earshot paid him no attention. After several minutes he stepped down and sought the padded pallet, where he stretched out with a groan. He hadn't realized until then how tired he was. He was very thirsty, but there was no water to drink in the room. There was an ornate pitcher and bowl on a small stand in the corner near the slop jar, but there was no water in either.

He closed his eyes, but a mental image of the obese tong leader was all he could visualize. The whole thing still seemed like some sort of nightmare. He rubbed a hand across his eyes. He didn't know how long he had been unconscious in the dungeon, but one does not rest well when oxygen-starved. A stubble of beard covered his face and his hair was matted. His eyes felt gritty and irritated. His skin was grainy with the salt of dried perspiration and his coat, which he had used for a pillow earlier, was missing. His wallet was still in his hip pocket and none of the few dollars was missing from it.

He lay back on the pallet and tried to sort out what was happening to him. He had been astonished when he saw the gold coins being poured out of one of the Wieland's Brewery beer kegs. Obviously, it was one of the kegs he had been hauling on his wagon. That explained why the two kidnappers had stolen his wagon at Cliff House. But how had the gold gotten there? Obviously, these robbers had had help from several people in the white community. Had the dock foreman who waved him off Saturday morning known about the coins hidden in the beer? Had the old man at the brewery, Carl Bauer, known about it? Maybe that was the reason he had cautioned Jay about not having anything happen to his load. Was it because he knew these Chinese would steal it? Or had Jay inadvertently been delivering it to someone else at Cliff House? The fat tong leader had said that the Chinese servants at Cliff House had deliberately set it afire just so they could steal the beer wagon in all the confusion. Did they really want him to lead them across Apache-infested country to the Mexican border with this load of stolen gold? It was incredible. It seemed to him that there were much easier and quicker ways of getting the loot out of the country. Carrying it away by ship would be an obvious one. Maybe too obvious. The Oriental mind was certainly not simple and direct. Otherwise, why all the elaborate pretense and roundabout maneuvering? But he had to admit, whatever their plan had been for getting the money away from the Mint and into Chinatown, it had worked. So far, so good. Now, if the fat one's story were true, the next step was to get it to Mexico to finance the lunatic's revolution in China.

With a start he realized the authorities were probably looking for him, since he had disappeared at the same time as the gold — *if* anyone had made a connection between the two. But he had not been near the Mint on Fifth Street. Why would they even connect his disappearance with the robbery? The tong leader had not told him precisely how the money had been stolen. As near as Jay could remember, he had hinted that there had been collusion with the assayer about the precise time and method of shipment. That meant that someone, either Chinese or hired whites, had probably robbed the shipment as it was leaving the Mint. But how? Even if the robbers knew where and when, weren't these shipments heavily guarded?

He had no idea how newly stamped gold coinage was shipped from the Mint. It was most likely taken by wagon to a train and then sent east, as bulky and heavy as this was likely to be. Why had he not heard about it before he went to Cliff House? It had to have occurred on Friday afternoon or night at the latest for the gold to have been taken to the brewery and hidden in the beer kegs, then loaded on his wagon for shipment to Cliff House. If it had happened sometime during the night on Friday, it might not have hit the papers on Saturday morning. A late-night shipment from the Mint by wagon might have been disguised as a routine delivery of some sort, and instead of being heavily guarded the authorities might have been relying on secrecy to haul the gold to the train depot. After all, what late revelers would look twice at a milk or bread wagon rolling through the streets of this city? But with advance knowledge of how, where, and when, with maybe a few hefty bribes thrown in . . . Well, somehow they had pulled it off. He wished he could get his hands on a newspaper to find out some of the details.

And what of his own fate? He hoped Fred Casey's instincts as a policeman would alarm him about Jay's disappearance. It must be Sunday morning. Maybe Fred would not miss him until he failed to show up at the Ferry House at the foot of Market Street for their trip across the bay to Oakland at one o'clock this afternoon.

He stood up on the low table and looked out the window again. The smell of fresh air coming through the glassless window was as heady as wine, even though tainted now and then with the odors of clogged drains and garbage.

With a start he heard the bolt slide open on the iron-backed wooden door to the room, and he sprang off the table and bounded across the room to flatten himself beside the doorway, ready to make a break or face whatever danger was coming.

CHAPTER 5

His heart was pounding as he listened to someone having trouble sliding the heavy bolt all the way back on the other side of the door. The door finally swung outward from the room and a young Chinese woman came in carrying a tray. As soon as she had taken two short steps into the room Jay was behind her and out the door before it could close. He was temporarily blind as he rushed into a darkened hallway. Before he could even begin to feel his way forward along the wall he heard a slight scuffling behind him. He whirled just as someone clamped both his arms to his sides in a crushing bearhug. He struggled wildly, but it was no use. He could smell the guard's cigarette breath as he was dragged back into the room. The future emperor of China was taking no chances on his escaping. Even though Jay had been considered one of the best wrestlers and all-around athletes in college, the guards the tong leader had posted on him were quick and tremendously strong. Another attempt at escape had ended before it really got started. He might have known they would not send a girl into his room alone without some sort of backup.

The burly guard threw him unceremoniously to the floor in the middle of the room, said something in Chinese to the girl who still stood holding the tray, and departed, closing, but not bolting, the door behind him.

The girl took the tray and set it on the low wooden table Jay had pulled against the wall to stand on.

"What is this?" Jay asked, coming over to the tray and removing the small towel that covered it. Jay was talking mostly to himself, since he assumed she knew no English.

"Food," she replied.

Startled, he looked around at her. "There is also some rice wine and water to drink." Her voice was almost musical in its delicacy, like the sound of wind chimes.

She made a slight bow and turned to go.

81

"Wait!" he cried, desperate for some-one to talk to. "What's your name?"

She paused, glancing at the closed door, then back at him. "Lee Sing," she said, hesitantly.

"What are you doing here? Do you work for Yen Ching?"

She shook her head. "I must go."

"Do you know I'm being held prisoner here?" he asked urgently, in a low voice.

She nodded.

Jay despaired as he looked at the beautiful oval face, the coal-black hair pulled back in a bun, and the slanted, downcast eyes. She was only a servant girl — a slave, probably, from the stories he had heard. The vast majority of women in Chinatown were. He was sur-prised that she could speak English. Perhaps she was the mistress of one of the tong leaders. But she would have no power or inclination to help him. He was wasting his time talking to her. A beau-tiful diversion in a silk kimono, a touch of humanity in this nightmare he had gotten caught up in. That was all she was, he decided, as she inclined her head again and turned toward the door.

"Won't you stay and talk to me while I eat?" he heard himself asking in an almost pleading voice.

"I will return later," she said over her shoulder in that soft, musical voice.

When the door closed behind her, Jay heard the heavy bolt slide into place. Then silence.

Jay sat down heavily on a cushion in the middle of the room. In his fatigue and fear he came as close as he had ever come to despair. Tears welled up in his eyes, and he began to feel very sorry for himself. But after a minute or two he pulled himself together. What was the matter with him? He had faced tough opponents before on the football grid-iron and the wrestling mats. Why was he being such a weakling now? After a few seconds of thought he put it down to fear of the unknown, and fatigue. Things always looked darker and more insurmountable when one was tired, run-down, and hungry. Then he remembered the food the girl had left.

He went over to the table and sat down on a cushion beside it to examine the contents of the tray. Some kind of very simple fare. A bowl containing some sort of meat mixed with rice, and a wooden spoon to eat it with. Not even a metal spoon or fork he might forge into a weapon, he thought as he picked it up. They've thought of everything.

The first thing he did was to drink most of the water in the pitcher without stopping. He had never tasted anything so good. Then he set to work on the rice and meat. By the time he had finished that he was beginning to feel somewhat better. Nothing like food to pick up one's energy and flagging spirits. He finished the water and then began tasting the rice wine. It was delicious. He got up and paced around the room as he sipped from the large china mug that held a good half-pint or more.

As he paced a disturbing thought occurred to him. The tong leader would not have revealed to him the information about the robbery, shown him the gold, and told him of his plans to headquarter in Mexico while financing a Chinese revolution if he didn't plan to kill Jay at the end of it all. The tong leader would want to avoid having Jay tell any or all of this to the law or the U.S. Secret Service, who were no doubt on the case by now. It was a chilling prospect. But then maybe the Chinese leader, whatever else he might be — such as a fanatical, half-cracked despot

— might just be a man of his word. It was a long shot, but maybe Jay could succeed in getting the gold and however many Chinese would accompany him across the desert into Mexico, be paid his reward and let go. But there were many things that could go wrong. It was all too tenuous. As meticulously planned and executed as this robbery had been, he couldn't help but think that the rest of the scheme would require the same careful planning.

He finished the rice wine and went toward the table to set down the mug. He began to feel hot and clammy, even though there was plenty of cool breeze coming through the window. Oh God, I hope that meat wasn't tainted, he thought. Or even poisoned. The thought made him sweat even worse. In a minute or so he knew something was definitely wrong. His head began to swim and he couldn't focus. He felt very weak, and he crawled on hands and knees toward the sleeping pallet to lie down. Then he passed out.

Jay heard the voice of an angel near his ear. He opened his eyes to darkness. I must have died and gone to heaven, he thought. He felt cool and comfortable and closed his eyes again. He felt so satisfied and sleepy. He just wanted to lie there and feel the cool air sweeping over him and hear the soft tinkling of the bell-like angel voice near him. What could be nicer?

Then he felt someone shake his shoulder, and he heard the voice again as he opened his eyes.

"Jay McGraw, get up and come with me."

It must be my guardian angel calling me to heaven, Jay thought. He had no sensation except one of extreme lethargy. A harder shake, and he began to wake up. Where was he? Then the thoughts of his captivity came rushing back on him, and he groaned again as his head began to pound. His mouth was dry and tasted terrible — as if the entire Chinese army had marched through it, barefoot. He almost smiled at his own joke, in spite of his misery.

"Jay McGraw." He heard his name spoken again by the melodic voice. He had never heard it spoken so sweetly.

"You must get up and come with me," she repeated. Lee Sing was kneeling beside him in the soft light of the coal-oil lamp she had lighted and set on the low table. He pushed himself up from the pallet to his hands and knees. His head throbbed anew. With an effort he staggered to his feet and leaned against the wall, pressing his face against the cool bricks.

"Come with me." She took his arm and led him toward the door. They went through it into the darkened hallway, and Jay was aware of the gorillalike guard following them in the shadows. No chance of making a break for it — not the way I feel, Jay thought. Even thinking was an effort. He felt as if he had been drugged, which no doubt he had. It must have been something in that rice wine. He felt like a fool: actually pleading with this girl to stay and talk with him while he ate and drank, and all the time her knowing she had drugged him.

She guided him to the end of the hallway, then turned right through a door and down a flight of stairs toward some subterranean room. His knees were so weak he had to grasp the bannister with both hands to keep from falling. Half of the Chinatown district must be below ground, Jay thought.

They went through another door that

opened out into a small, tiled room with what appeared to be a sunken bath in the middle of the floor. Another young woman, dressed in a flowered kimono, was standing there. Her slanted eyes were heavily made up and her mouth, in a pale, olive face, was painted in a perfect cupid's bow. Lee Sing quickly began to strip Jay of his sweat- and dirt-stained shirt. She threw it on the floor and then began unbuckling his belt. Jay instinctively reached for his pants. She shook her head and pointed to the water in the sunken tub.

"You must bathe before the ceremony," she said.

"What ceremony?"

"Come. We haven't much time." She quickly pulled down his trousers and underwear.

"*I* can do it," Jay said, turning away from her, embarrassed. "Nobody's given me a bath since I was a little baby."

Both girls still stood there, watching. "Well, what the hell," he muttered, kicking out of his pants and slipping quickly into the three-foot-deep water. "If you're going to stay and watch so I don't escape, I'd better get underwater."

Lee Sing quickly slipped out of her

kimono and stepped into the warm water beside him, wearing only the bottoms of some sort of silk underdrawers. She had a petite, but perfect, figure. She took a bottle of perfumed soap at tub side and began to rub it on his shoulders and arms.

Jay squirmed under her touch and could feel himself becoming embarrassingly aroused.

"I can do it, thank you," he said firmly, taking the bottle from her hand and turning away from her.

"It is the Chinese custom," she said.

"It is not our custom," he said emphatically, sliding down under the water to scrub his fingers through his hair. He bathed quickly, trying not to look at her. She climbed out of the pool before he did, dried herself, and dressed. She held out a large towel for him when he was ready to step up. The other young woman had withdrawn discreetly to the far side of the room, where she busied herself arranging various bottles and lotions on a shelf. Lee Sing was businesslike and unconcerned, hardly looking at him as she handed him some clean clothing that consisted of undershorts, black cotton, Chinese-style trousers, and a loose, white cotton jumper top that he slipped over his head. He retrieved his belt, wallet, comb, and loose change from his own pants pockets. There was a mirror on the far wall, and he went to comb his hair. After straightening his dark hair he rubbed a hand over the stubble on his face.

"No razor now," she said, shaking her head.

No weapons, you mean, Jay thought, smiling weakly at her. She met his eyes for the first time, and Jay was sure a trace of a smile passed over her face. But he never let the thought cross his mind that this lovely Oriental girl was the least bit friendly toward him. She was here to do a job on somebody's orders. The girl then took his hand and led him back up the stairs. The gorilla-guard was lurking in the darkness, smoking a cigarette. Jay felt a rush of cool air as someone down the hall opened a door to the outside. The clothes he wore were loose and comfortable but they felt strange on him. He wore his own short boots.

"Where are we going?" Jay asked, when they paused in a hallway under an overhead coal-oil lamp that bathed this portion of the passageway in yellow light.

Lee Sing glanced around and saw that the guard was out of earshot several yards away, leaning against the wall. She stepped closer to Jay and spoke quietly. "You are going to be initiated as a *boo how doy* in the Chee Kong tong at midnight."

The words sent a chill of terror up Jay's back. A boo how doy, Fred Casey had explained to him, was a hatchet man of the tong.

"Why? I am not Oriental. I don't even speak Chinese. And most of all I am not a killer."

"It is on the special order of Yen Ching that you are to become a member of this secret society tonight. Since you have been chosen for a mission that is so important to our cause, this will bind you ever closer to your brothers in the tong, so that you will never betray us. You will be bound by a blood oath to others in the Chee Kong tong. Two others are to be initiated tonight with you, but the questions will be put to you in English. Time is short, so listen and remember the responses that I will tell you. You must know the responses when you are questioned."

For the next ten minutes she drilled him in the ceremony that was about to take place and in the questions that would be asked of him and the traditional answers. The whole thing sounded like a lot of juvenile mumbo jumbo. It reminded him of some of the secret clubs he and his friends had formed when they were children. But these were grown men, serious enough to hire assassins to cleave the skulls of members of similar secret clubs. If he hadn't been so nervous he would have laughed out loud.

"Will you be there to coach me?" he finally asked.

"Oh no. I am not allowed inside. I have never witnessed one of these ceremonies. My master has coached me on all that will happen. Now you must repeat the answers to be sure you have them correct."

So they went through the procedure and the questioning again, until Jay felt reasonably comfortable that he had it right.

"If you can't go in with me, why were you sent to coach me?" Jay asked.

"Because my master taught me English," she replied simply.

He looked at the girl again. Undoubtedly, she was the concubine of the disgusting, obese creature he had seen earlier. How did she stand it? Apparently, she was a slave and had no choice. At least she was not one of the "sing-song" girls in one of the houses of ill repute that were so common in Chinatown.

A door near them swung open and two men stepped out. Jay noted that the door was backed with iron.

"These two men will accompany you," the girl said. "They know just enough English to get you through the ceremony."

She was standing next to him and, unseen by anyone, gave his hand a gentle squeeze. Then she was walking quickly away from him, and his two escorts guided him into the semidarkness of the room to become a "blood brother" of the Chee Kong, the most powerful tong in Chinatown.

CHAPTER 6

They entered a low-ceilinged room
whose walls reeked of mildew. Jay had
been instructed by Lee Sing that one of
his two male escorts would act as his
mother and one as his father in the
ritual ceremony. A group of men squat-
ted on their heels, solemnly facing an
improvised altar at one end of the room.

Jay was led to a corner and, for the
second time tonight, was told to strip off
all his clothes. But because of the young
woman's forewarnings he was not surprised, and he quickly stripped naked.
His body was carefully examined for
birthmarks, of which he was free. Just
what this had to do with anything Lee
Sing couldn't tell him. She only knew it
was part of the ceremony.

Jay was then allowed to pull on his
trousers and go forward to meet the
Grand Master of Ceremonies. The man
looked nothing like Yen Ching. This man

was lean, with a face pitted by smallpox scars. He also had a disfiguring knife scar that angled down from his forehead, across his cheekbone to the corner of his mouth. Jay wondered if he had somehow survived an attack by a hatchet man.

This man eyed Jay and then looked down at a paper in his hand, apparently to help him with his English.

"Have you carefully considered the step you are about to take?" he asked.

"Yes, Reverend Scribe," Jay answered.

"Are you ready to storm the Great Wall?"

"Quite ready, Reverend Scribe," Jay answered.

"Have you been prepared with weapons?"

"Not as yet."

"How can a child be born without a mother?"

"My revered mother accompanies me, Reverend Scribe," Jay responded, indicating the Chinaman at his side. "She stands upon my left, and my godfather stands upon my right."

"Are you ready to become a blood brother?" the scarred one asked.

"All ready, Reverend Scribe."

"Then let your mother proceed to shed the blood of maternity."

Jay was then led to the altar. On it were the symbols of the Chee Kong tong Lee Sing had told him to expect. There he saw small dishes of sugar to remove all bitterness from the heart and a dish of oil so all could have light in the future, and a bowl of vinegar into which the blood of the initiates would be mixed.

Jay's "godfather" pricked Jay's finger with a needle. As it dripped blood he plunged it into the bowl of vinegar, stirring it. Jay felt a sharp sting as he watched the two other newcomers doing the same. Then each of the three placed his finger in his mouth and sucked it dry before stating loudly, "Thou art my blood brother!" Of course the other two said it in Chinese, just as the Grand Master of ceremonies had questioned them in their native tongue. All of the men in the room shouted "Ho!" or something that sounded like it, in unison, like a loud "Amen!" to the end of a prayer.

Jay was led before the Grand Master again and ordered by one of his escorts, in halting English, to kowtow three times. Jay got down on his knees and touched his forehead to the floor three times.

Then, in order to test his personal courage, he was ordered to walk between two lines of men with drawn swords. As he passed between them they dropped the swords onto his naked shoulders. But at the last possible instant each man turned his sharp blade so that the flat part of it fell on the skin.

Then the Grand Master went into a long harangue in Chinese, none of which Jay understood. Next the man tried reading something in English for his benefit. It was poorly written and poorly read, but he gathered it had something to do with the objectives of the tong, directions on diet and behavior, and coming to the aid of any brother tong member. It emphasized the widespread activities of the tong and ended with the words, "Bear also in mind that while the Chee Kong tong protects it also punishes, and should you prove traitorous to our cause your blood shall pollute the soil of the land. Be you where you may, the Chee Kong tong will find you out."

After this warning Jay and the other two initiates took oaths to observe these instructions. Then, in the grand finale of the ceremony, Jay swore in English, "Should I prove untrue to my promise, may my life be dashed out of my body as I now dash the blood from this bowl." The other two swore the same in Chinese. With that the three of them raised bowls of chicken blood and hurled them to the floor, where they shattered. The ceremony was now over and Jay McGraw, son of the Midwest, had become a reluctant boo how doy, a hatchet man of the Chee Kong tong.

He was given his white jumper, which he put back on, and was sent out the door into the hallway where Lee Sing awaited him. She scrutinized his face for his reaction to what had just taken place.

For some reason Jay was beginning to feel that this girl was the only one he could trust in all this madness. She took his hand and led him back toward his room.

"Do you feel different now?" she asked.

Jay shook his head. "That was the silliest damn thing I've ever seen. It reminded me of what I've heard of some of the stupid things that go on during college fraternity initiations."

Whether she was shocked, relieved, or just disinterested in this answer, he couldn't tell from her face. She never changed expression.

The ever-present guard slid back the bolt on the door of his room, and he and Lee Sing entered. She lighted a coal-oil lamp that contained a perfumed oil and set it on his low table. If the ceremony had started at midnight, Jay guessed it now had to be after 1:00 A.M. Jay wondered if Yen Ching actually thought he would take this silly initiation seriously. Apparently the Chinese in the tong did, as did the members of other tongs in Chinatown. As informed as he thought he was about white man's customs, Yen Ching was sadly mistaken if he thought a compulsory oath or two would make Jay McGraw suddenly embrace a murderous tong.

Lee Sing stood looking around the room, and Jay wondered what would come next. Would she bring him more food and water and maybe some drugged wine to keep him well under control for a few more hours? Or would she simply leave and lock him in for the rest of the night?

"Jay McGraw," she began, and he

thrilled again at the sound of his name from her melodic voice. "Do you wish to be a member of the Chee Kong tong?"

"A forced oath from a captive does not make a good tong member," he rejoined, "any more than if a Chinese man were dragged from here and taken to court and forced to swear an oath of allegiance to the United States of America as a naturalized citizen."

She nodded, seeming to take a more personal interest in him than she had previously. She looked closely at him, and began to say something further, but stopped. Finally she said, "I will bring you more food and water in the morning."

Without a backward glance she went out the door and slid the bolt.

CHAPTER 7

Jay was thankful that the cold sea fog coming through his open window awakened him sometime before dawn. He had no coat and no covering and, tired as he was, the damp chill roused him on his sleeping pallet while it was still dark outside.

He rolled over and sat up, shivering, and started to reach for the lamp on the table when he heard a crash and a shout from somewhere in the building. Then there were voices shouting in high-pitched Chinese and the sound of running feet. Startled, he fumbled for a match to light the lamp but then remembered he had none. He sat in the dark, wondering what was going on. A fight? Was the building on fire? If so, would anyone remember he was in here? The thought tightened his stomach. Then he heard what sounded like someone pounding on a door somewhere above him. More yelling and the clash of steel, and then two gunshots.

He was on his feet in the darkness and jumped up onto the small table to look out the window. He could see no one in the alley. The fog and the darkness blanketed anyone who might have been there. The only thing he could make out was the reflection of a faint glow of gaslight from the street lamp at one end of the alley.

He heard the thunder of many running feet on a wooden floor somewhere overhead, then a fusillade of gunshots.

A sudden thought struck him: Maybe this was a police raid. Maybe he would be rescued.

In a sudden lull in the noise, he heard the bolt slide back on the door to his room. His throat constricted and he flattened himself against the wall, hoping whoever it was could not see him in the dark. A shadowy figure entered, carrying no lamp. He held his breath, ready to fight or run. The figure came straight toward his sleeping pallet.

"Jay McGraw!" The low, melodic sound of that voice was literally music to his ears. He let out his breath in a rush.

"Lee Sing! What is it?"

"The Hip Yee and Po Sang tongs have broken into our building and their boo how doy are trying to kill Yen Ching. Come quickly!" She grabbed his hand in the darkness and led him toward the door.

"Where?"

She stopped so suddenly that he almost ran into her.

"If I help you escape from here, will you help me?" she asked urgently.

His heart leapt with joy. "Yes! Yes! Let's go!" he almost shouted.

She didn't move. "Promise me you will not let the tong take me back. I would be severely punished or killed for my transgression."

"Nothing will happen to you. I promise."

"Then come quickly. I know a way that our people escape from the police raids."

Jay noticed that she paused to shut and bolt the door behind them when they left. A good precaution, he thought, in case the guard or anyone else came by. They would not know immediately that he was gone.

She led him on a twisting, winding course through the building, up staircases lit by dim lamps. He was amazed at her athletic grace and endurance as she bounded up the steps two at a time ahead of him. He noticed she was wearing long white cotton trousers under the straight garment that was split up both sides to the hips.

On the second flight of steps she suddenly stopped and threw herself back against the wall, and Jay did likewise as four guards dressed in quilted armor swept past them down the stairs, cleavers and knives in hand.

Then they were at the top of the stairs and running down a hallway. She suddenly skidded to a halt in front of him, grabbed his arm, and yanked him into a room, shutting the door.

"Boo how doy!" she panted. "The Hip Yee tong men!"

Jay wished he had a weapon of some kind but he felt helpless. More than for a weapon, he wished to be out of here and free. But it was all up to this slender girl to accomplish that. She stood in front of him, peering carefully out the door she held open a crack.

"They are trying to kill everyone in the building as well as Yen Ching, to break the power of the Chee Kong tong," she whispered, her breath coming in gasps.

With a start Jay realized that he was now a member of that tong — not that anyone would stop to ask before impaling him on the end of a dagger.

"Now! It is clear. Come!"

He followed her out of the empty room as she ran in her light slippers to the end of the hall. It appeared to be a dead end. She leaned her shoulder against the wall and pushed.

"Help!" she panted.

Jay gave the wall a push and a portion of the wall pivoted. They slipped inside and she paused to push the panel back into place. She fumbled for his hand in the inky blackness. It was suddenly very quiet. The shouting seemed a long way away. She was feeling her way along with no light but apparently knew where she was and where she was leading him. After about ten steps she stopped.

"There. Above. We must reach that."

Jay looked up. A faint rectangular patch of light was directly over his head.

"We must climb," she said urgently. "Quickly. Someone else will be coming. Others know of this passage."

Jay felt around in the darkness. How

was he to get up there? If he could only see! He looked up again. The small rectangular patch of faint light was the foggy sky above the building. It was about the size of a large chimney, he estimated. It was at least twenty feet above him.

"Here." She led him to the lath and plaster wall. They were in some sort of dead space between inside walls. He felt in the blackness and his hands encountered an upright wooden frame, then another about two feet away. Someone had made a rough ladder.

"Hurry!" she pleaded. "Someone is coming!"

"You go first." Jay's hands virtually encircled her waist as he lifted her to the second rung of the ladder and he was struck by her slimness. She scrambled up the ladder in the dark like a cat up a tree. Jay was right behind her. He had gone up only two steps, feeling his way with his feet and hands, when the secret panel swung open and light from the hallway poured in, followed by excited Chinese voices. Others trying to escape, Jay thought. One of the men carried a lantern high as several figures entered the space. A low scream from Lee Sing above him made Jay look up and then down quickly. These were not Chee Kong tong men escaping; these were Hip Yee tong men attacking. Jay leapt up one more rung just as a meat cleaver splintered the wooden rung where his foot had been. He clawed his way frantically up several feet to the opening in the roof, jabbing several splinters into his hands from the rough wood as he did so. With Lee Sing pulling at him he squeezed through the narrow opening in the roof. He looked around quickly for something to block the hole with but nothing presented itself.

"This way!" Lee Sing led him nimbly over the tarred roof to the edge of the building, where the brick wall that jutted up about two feet almost abutted the upthrust brick wall of the next building. They leapt up onto the low wall and across, running carefully, Jay trying his best to follow directly behind the girl. In the chill fog of early dawn about all he could see, when she got a few yards ahead, was a flash of white from the cotton trousers moving under the kimono. He wanted to look back to see if they were being pursued but dared not for fear of falling, as she led him diagonally down the slope of a canted roof. My boots aren't the best kind of footwear for this sort of thing Jay thought, panting along in her wake.

Suddenly he caught his toe on a projecting low vent he hadn't seen and pitched headlong, a sickening feeling in the pit of his stomach as he flew through the void, arms outstretched in front of his face. He hit the slope of the tarred roof and slid several feet facedown until his hands shot out into space. He clutched wildly at the metal gutter that had caught his jumper sleeve. The rest of his body slid to a stop, one arm and leg hanging over the edge.

"Jay McGraw! Are you all right?"

He hardly dared breathe, much less answer. He grunted, and she crept carefully down the steep pitch of roof. She touched his back but did not try to take hold of him. There was no way she could get enough grip with her slippers. And slight as she was she could never pull Jay's one hundred and seventy pounds back from the void.

"Be careful, Lee Sing," Jay hissed through clenched teeth. "Don't touch me or I may fall. How high is it here?"

She hesitated. "About three stories.

Maybe two. I am not sure."

"What's below me?"

Again she hesitated. "There is an alley below. With paving stones. But there may be a balcony or two on this side." She paused, then said, "If you can slide along just a little way, there is an iron ladder down the side of the building. That is where I was going when you fell."

Jay tensed his body and tried to shift his weight ever so slightly. It was nearly impossible. By hugging the roof with his left arm and leg and half of his body and head he could remain where he was — with the help of his left boot heel at the end of a crooked leg, jammed into the metal gutter. But as soon as he tried to move he could feel himself becoming overbalanced.

"Which way, Lee Sing, forward or backward?"

"Backward."

Jay groaned. "I was afraid you were going to say that." He was sweating profusely in spite of the chill, damp fog.

"Lee, I can't move. Get down the ladder and run for the nearest police station. Ask for a man named Fred Casey."

"Fred Casey?"

"Yes. Tell him I sent you and tell him

what happened to me. I can't get up from here and I can't slide backward. I'll have to swing down and drop off. It's the only way I have of getting down without a ladder. I'm going to be hurt, or maybe killed. If I make it, I will see you later. Go! Get the police and tell them you must see Fred Casey. Don't tell your story to anyone else! Hurry! The tong may be chasing us."

"No. I cannot leave you here."

He was sweating worse, and his hands were getting wet both from perspiration and the fog. He had to make a move soon or fall. He was desperate. "Lee Sing, go down the ladder and wait for me below in the alley. I will be down in a minute one way or another. Then run for help."

She touched him lightly and moved away toward the ladder, hugging the steep pitch of the roof.

Jay forced himself to wait a full minute, counting the seconds. Then he took a deep breath, unhooked his left heel from the gutter, gripped the gutter with his right hand, and let his body slide over the edge. As he went down he caught the edge of the gutter with his left hand and hung, full length, facing the brick wall. The gutter bent slightly.

He prayed it was not too old and rusted. It would have to hold his weight as he inched his way to his left. Lee Sing had said the iron ladder was only a short distance away. How far?

Suddenly he heard a slight ripping as some of the old fastenings let go, and he felt the gutter sagging. His stomach tightened and he stopped moving. The gutter appeared to he holding, so again he carefully slid his hands a few more inches. So far so good. He made about three feet, then four. He slid his left hand over, then brought his right hand along. He didn't know how long he had been hanging, but his arms were beginning to ache. How far was that ladder? He shifted his hands again. With a loud ripping noise the gutter tore loose. In an instant of panic he knew he was gone! But he hung on instinctively as the gutter let him swing down with it. Just as his hands slipped off and he started to fall, his feet and knees crashed into something that gave under him with a tearing noise. He had torn through a canvas awning a few feet below the edge of the roof and landed on a balcony, crushing a wicker chair in the process. He scrambled to his feet, checking himself quickly for damage and thankful to be alive. Except for some bruises and his hands being raw he seemed to be none the worse for his experience.

"Jay McGraw!"

He jumped back amid the clutter of broken furniture at the sound of his own name. Then he realized it was Lee Sing's voice. He peered into the darkness.

"Here!"

He leaned over the edge of the balcony and saw her, not six feet away, clinging to the side of the building. She was on the iron ladder.

"Can you reach this?"

Jay gauged the distance from where he was to the white blur in the murk. Even stretching he was less than five feet eleven inches tall, with an appropriate reach. And even in good light it would have been very difficult to stretch that far. He took a deep, shuddering breath. He would have to try.

"Hurry! Someone is coming!"

Jay heard the feet sliding and clumping over the roof above him. He quickly climbed over the railing and, gripping the bannister with his right hand, reached as far as he could along the wall with his left. He was about a foot or more short.

"Lee Sing, go down the ladder. I'll have to jump for it."

Without a word she did as she was told and disappeared into the darkness below. He kept his eyes on the spot where he had seen her hands. There was one of the rungs. He pulled himself back to the railing, coiled his body, and launched himself toward that spot.

His wrist banged an iron rung and he clutched at it as he fell, scrabbling with his boot toes against the brick wall. His damp fingers caught, then slipped off the iron. His chin connected with the next one as he slid down, but then his hands found the rung and held it, nearly wrenching his arms out of their sockets as his full weight swung beneath. Then he got his feet under him and stood there a moment, gasping. He had made it. But he had no time to be relieved, as Chinese voices sounded just above him. Friend or foe, he didn't know and didn't care. None of the people here would be his friend except Lee Sing. The adrenaline was pumping, and he quickly climbed down and found Lee Sing.

"This way!" She took his hand and they

ran, the chill wind fanning his sweaty body. Jay let her lead. She knew these back alleys and twisting passageways, even in the gray light of early dawn. He was just thankful to have his feet back on solid ground. They saw no one in the streets as they ran past the gas street lamps that made fuzzy balls of light in the fog.

This girl is in good condition, Jay thought after they had run for several blocks. They finally left the Chinese quarter and she slowed to a walk, breathing heavily. Jay, too, was winded as they walked along, not talking.

"There is a police house close by?" she finally asked.

Jay looked around. It was still very foggy, but the gray light was filtering through by now well enough for him to make out a few things.

"Yes. The California Street station is not far."

They started jogging again, this time with Jay leading the way. He had his bearings now. He had accompanied Fred Casey here once when Fred was on his way to turn in a report, and he thought he remembered passing this way a time or two while on one of his deliveries.

CHAPTER 8

"So it's Fred Casey you're wantin', is it?" the Irish desk sergeant said when Jay and Lee Sing gasped out their request to him a few minutes later in the station house. "And why would you be wantin' him? Can't someone here help you two?" He leaned back in his chair behind the high desk. He wore an immaculate dark-blue uniform coat with a silver badge pinned to it.

"Fred Casey's a friend of mine, and I have to see him. It's urgent!" Jay said again.

"Well, if that's the way of it. . . ." He swiveled in his wooden chair. "Any of you lads know what shift Fred Casey's working?" he yelled at the three other men in the room.

"Yeah, Sarge. He's on the Chinatown squad. I think he just went over to the night shift. Let me check the schedule. Yeah, here it is. He's on duty now.

Should be gettin' off in an hour or so," one of the men answered.

"You won't give me a hint as to what this is all about?" the desk sergeant asked again.

"I'd rather tell my story to Casey," Jay insisted.

"Joe, how about runnin' along and see if you might fetch this Fred Casey. Don't be too long if you can't find him."

"Right, Sarge." The uniformed patrolman started out.

"And don't be all day about it," the sergeant called after him as he sauntered out the front door. The man broke into a jog.

"You two want to have a seat on the bench over there? You look pretty winded. You've been doin' a bit of running yourselves."

Jay nodded as he sank down gratefully on the nearby bench.

"Can I get you two something? Maybe some coffee?"

"That would be great."

"What about your Chinese friend? I don't have any tea."

"I would like some coffee, please," Lee Sing answered for herself.

The big sergeant's eyebrows went up

at the sound of her perfect English.

"Jay! My God, where have you been?" Fred Casey cried as he came in the front door a half hour later. The black-haired policeman glanced curiously at Lee Sing.

"Fred, is there a place we can talk privately?"

"Sarge, I'm going to question these people."

The sergeant nodded and pointed at a side door.

Jay and Lee Sing followed Casey into the other room. Jay was tired, but the hot coffee with sugar was beginning to revive him.

"What the hell happened to you?" Casey asked when he had closed the door.

"Fred, you're not going to believe this, but every word of it is true," Jay began, and proceeded to tell him the whole story from the time he'd picked up his load at Wieland's Brewery to deliver to Cliff House.

Fred Casey sat and listened without interrupting, occasionally biting at the corners of his black mustache.

When he'd finished, Casey whistled softly. "You've had yourself quite a weekend. I had turned in a missing person report on you but didn't have much hope of that doing any good, since it appeared you had run off with a wagonload of your employer's beer. A few people I questioned out at Cliff House remembered seeing you, but they didn't know where you had gone. The ironic thing about it is, I was walking my beat hardly three blocks from where I believe you were being held.

"Yes, you're right about that gold robbery. This city has been in an uproar since it was discovered Saturday. Most of us have been put on overtime, trying to locate the gold. The federal agents have been swarming all over the place. Trouble is, nobody knows where to look. Or at least they didn't until now. God, I wonder if it's too late?" He chewed thoughtfully at the corner of his mustache.

"Too late for what?"

"To find that gold. Lee Sing, can you lead us back to that building?"

She nodded, her eyes going wider, Jay thought, with fear. And he remembered his promise to protect her so that she would never have to go back to enslavement.

"Good. We have no time to lose. I just hope they haven't already moved it, or that it was stolen by that Hip Yee tong." He jumped out of his chair. "Do you want to come with us, or aren't you up to it right now?" he asked Jay.

"I'll come." If Lee Sing was guiding them, he was sticking as close to her side as possible. He could never do enough to repay her for saving his life.

Word was sent to police headquarters by a police courier. By the time a messenger reached the home of the police commissioner to roust him out of bed, a force of twenty-five well-armed men had been formed and was advancing on Chinatown. But all this had taken over an hour, in addition to the half hour or so that Jay and Lee Sing had waited for Fred Casey to be found. Jay estimated it had been over two hours since the raid on the Chee Kong tong headquarters had begun. If the doors to the outside of the building had been faced with iron as had some of the interior doors, he wondered how men armed only with hatchets and cleavers and revolvers had breached them. Maybe a door had been left unbolted or they had found a window that had no bars. It was idle speculation. They *had* gotten in. As he rode in the paddy wagon with Lee Sing and Fred Casey into the bowels of the dreaded Chinese quarter, he wondered to himself what had become of Yen Ching and the gold.

Compared to the time it had taken them to run out of danger, it seemed to take no time at all to return to it. It was only a few minutes before the driver was pulling up in front of a building Jay did not recognize.

"This is it," Lee Sing said, sitting very still inside the wagon and nervously wringing her hands on her lap. Then Jay realized the reason he didn't recognize the place was that he had never seen the front of the building. He had been taken in from an alleyway and had escaped through the roof and out the back.

The police quickly surrounded the place. A few early rising passersby and Chinese merchants viewed the proceedings from afar.

On orders from Fred Casey Jay and Lee Sing remained inside the paddy wagon as the raid commenced. Jay had a sinking feeling when he saw the officers break in the front door with no trouble at all. He could hear their feet pounding on the stairs inside. Seven or eight officers remained outside, loosely surrounding the building, their guns drawn in case anyone tried to escape. Lee Sing had told them about the escape hatch in the roof, and three men had been dispatched up the iron fire escape to the roof to cut off any retreat in that direction.

In less than fifteen minutes the uniformed and plain clothes lawmen came drifting out, one and two at a time to stand on the sidewalk, talking. A tall captain came over to the paddy wagon and looked in the back door at Jay and Lee Sing.

"The building is empty but there's been a helluva fight: furniture and woodwork all hacked, fresh blood barely dried on the floors, doors busted in, but not a soul in sight. Would you two mind coming with me to show us exactly where you talked to this Yen Ching and where the gold was?"

The captain handed the Chinese girl down the step of the wagon, and the three of them went inside the building. Jay immediately had a trapped, closed-in feeling as he entered the dim hallways. Lee Sing was evidently feeling it too, because she pressed close to his side. Since Jay had been led blindfolded, with a sack over his head, he had no idea where Yen Ching's plush hall had been, but Lee Sing led them up the stairs and directly to it. The door had been fearfully hacked, and splintered wood hung from the door frame. The iron door had not given, but the policemen had finally forced it open with pry bars far enough to allow one person at a time into the big room. They passed single file into the room, and Jay saw Fred Casey talking to a plainclothesman. Fred came over immediately.

"Doesn't look like the raiders got in here," Fred said. "We finished forcing the door. Everything's still in good order. Nothing broken. No blood."

Jay briefly described Yen Ching again. "He was sitting, or half lying, in that big chair on the raised platform at the end of the room," he finished. "A couple of his guards brought in the gold from a room back behind that throne."

Jay followed Fred and the captain to the door he had just described. It opened into a small five-sided, brick-walled room with a heavy iron door. When Jay stepped into the room the men's voices suddenly sounded dead, as if the room swallowed up sound. It appeared to be built better and stronger than any other part of the building he had seen. A perfect vault. Whether that had been its original purpose or not he didn't know. This headquarters building of the Chee Kong tong appeared to have been built in different stages and added onto haphazardly. But this room looked to be a safe retreat from anything, in or near the center of the complex of rooms and hallways and stairways. The place was a real firetrap, Jay thought, with its wooden floors and steps and furniture, barred windows and iron doors and smoky lamps. It was a wonder to him it hadn't caught fire during the raid.

But there was one thing about this room that accounted for the fact that Yen Ching and the gold had disappeared: while the door to the adjacent large room remained locked, a four-foot-square lift was set flush in the middle of the floor.

"Our men have been through this entire building, from the lowest subterranean dungeon to the roof," the tall captain was saying, "and they've vanished without a trace — and taken the gold with them. If, indeed, there *was* any gold," he added significantly, glancing at Jay.

Jay felt his face begin to redden at the insinuation. The room was completely empty. He wished there had been at least one coin or one Wieland's Brewery keg to verify his story. But somehow they had all gotten away, and taken the gold with them.

"That lift set in the floor there could easily have let down the big fat Chinaman and all the gold. Probably would have taken more than one trip to do it, but that elevator's cables and pulleys are all oiled up and look to have been in frequent use. It goes down three floors to ground level. From there it's anybody's guess where they went. I'd say we probably didn't miss them by much more than an hour. Maybe if we're lucky we can still get them."

They walked back out into the big hall. It seemed to Jay that it had been weeks since he had stood on this very same green and gold carpet listening to an obese lunatic describing his plans for overthrowing the Manchu rulers of China. He shook his head. It all seemed so unreal now. He was very tired, and longed to lie down in a bed somewhere and sleep for about ten hours. He glanced at Lee Sing. She didn't show it, but she had to be as fatigued as he was.

The captain was at the door of the room talking to two men in dark wool suits who had just entered. Jay couldn't hear what they were saying, but several times the uniformed captain turned and gestured in his direction. By the tone of the voices and the looks on their faces the newcomers appeared to be very irritated with whatever the captain was telling them.

Another more thorough search of the premises took the police another half hour while Jay and Lee Sing waited outside. Then a guard was placed on the building and the paddy wagon, with Fred Casey, Jay McGraw, and Lee Sing inside, pulled away and headed back for the station house.

"Maybe if I hadn't insisted on waiting for someone to find you we could have caught them and recovered that gold," Jay said, leaning his elbows dejectedly on his knees.

"Maybe. Maybe not," Fred replied. "A cordon of police is being thrown up around Chinatown, and every pedestrian and wagon that leaves the district will be searched. They may have already left the city with it. But frankly it would be my guess that it's still hidden somewhere in the Chinese quarter."

"Who were those two men who came in and were talking to the captain?" Jay asked. "They didn't look like your detectives."

"Secret Service men. They were pretty angry that they weren't called from their hotel earlier. I don't know what they could have done. Just jurisdictional pride. They'll probably catch hell from their superiors in Washington for not being in on the initial raid with us, even though the horses had already bolted from the barn. I'm glad I'm not high enough to get into all those political rows." He grinned. "Cheer up, man. It wasn't your fault they got away. At least now we know where the gold *was*, which is more than anyone knew before. I'm just damn glad to have you back in one piece." He slapped Jay on the shoulder. "Even if you do look a little Oriental in that garb."

Jay finally grinned back at him. "I'm just tired and can't think straight. I don't think your captain believes there was ever any gold there."

"He's just frustrated. And he's been trained to consider all possibilities, including lying witnesses. You wouldn't believe the number of cranks who've given us false leads since this story hit the newspapers."

"Well, to hell with it for now," Jay said. "I have to go back and face my boss and try to explain to him what happened to his wagon and team and his load of steam beer. What am I supposed to tell him? For all I know he may be in on this whole plot. After all, that gold had to get into those kegs somehow, most likely at the brewery. I don't know. My head's in a whirl. If it's all right with you I think I'll go home to my rooming house and get some sleep."

Fred Casey frowned. "That may be dangerous. If they knew that much about you they know where you live. I'm off duty now. I'll take you to my place for now. We'll discuss this when you're rested. I have tonight off, unless they call me for overtime duty."

"What about Lee Sing?" Jay asked. "I promised her I'd protect her from going back to that slavery."

Casey sat back in the wagon that was

bouncing over the cobblestones. He chewed thoughtfully on the corner of his black mustache. "That may be more of a problem than guarding you," he said.

CHAPTER 9

"Mrs. Frierson, this girl needs protection and a safe place to live for a time," Fred Casey was saying about an hour later as he, Lee Sing, and Jay sat in the parlor of the Methodist Mission about three blocks from Chinatown. Even though it was only nine o'clock in the morning, Mrs. Emily Frierson was dressed in a starched white, ruffled blouse, with a high neck and a cameo pin at the throat and a long, straight gray skirt that swept the floor. Her dark hair was piled high on her head and she wore silver, wire-rimmed spectacles. A woman in her thirties, she and her husband had lived in San Francisco only three years, but she had almost single-handedly organized a campaign to throw sand into the well-oiled machinery of the Chinese slave-girl trade.

She took off her glasses, polished them on a handkerchief, and held them to the light streaming in through the bay windows of the big house. The fog was finally beginning to burn away outside. She replaced her spectacles and regarded Lee Sing through them.

"Of course. There is no question but that she will have a safe haven here. Does she speak English at all?"

"Yes, I speak English very well," Lee Sing replied for herself.

"Excellent."

"Then we'll leave her in your capable hands," Casey said, rising from the horsehair sofa and moving toward the front door. Mrs. Frierson followed him as he stepped out onto the small porch.

"Take extra precautions with this one," he said quietly. "She may be an important witness in one of the largest robberies in this country's history — that is, if we can locate the gold from the Mint."

Her hazel eyes widened slightly but all she said was, "We'll be very careful. Don't worry."

"Lee Sing, I'll come by to see you tomorrow," Jay was saying to the girl, who was still inside the parlor. He took her hands. "You saved my life. Thank you. You can stay here until the robbers of the Chee Kong tong are caught and the gold recovered. If they're not, you can decide where you want to go and what you want to do. You are free from the slavery of Yen Ching now."

A trace of a smile crossed Lee Sing's beautiful, cameolike face. "Jay McGraw, you are a good man," she said simply. She stepped forward, put her arms around his waist, and hugged him.

He was taken aback. "I . . . I'll see you tomorrow, then."

"Yes." She smiled again as she stepped back.

With a nod to Mrs. Frierson, he followed Fred down off the porch and they proceeded up the street, walking back to the California Street station house a few blocks away.

"What is your opinion of this whole business?" Casey asked after a long silence.

"Damned if I know. As farfetched as it sounds I guess it could be true."

"I wonder if they actually did get the gold?"

"I told you I saw it."

"You saw a pile of gold coins that were minted this year and were uncirculated. You didn't see all of it. Three million dollars' worth of double eagles would be ungodly heavy. Probably weigh in the neighborhood of four tons or better."

"Damn! Never thought of that. But why would they show me several thousand dollars' worth of new gold coins and claim it was part of the robbery if it wasn't?"

Fred shook his head. "I don't know. Just thinking out loud and exploring the possibilities. Jay, we've known each other only a couple of months, but I believe and trust you. I believe everything you've said about what happened. The problem is, I don't know if the people who captured you were telling the truth. If they did in fact get the gold, maybe this Yen Ching pumped you full of a farfetched tale and then made sure you escaped to tell the law."

"Why would he do that?"

Casey shrugged. "Maybe to throw everyone off the track so they could take the gold somewhere else."

"But it makes no sense. Why all the elaborate scheming? Why was I even involved in it?"

"Well, let me start from the beginning and give you my reasoning behind this. Here's the way I've got it figured out. I may be entirely wrong, but just hear me out and then give me your opinion. First of all, the government contracts with Wells Fargo and Company to transport their gold. The two heavy, reinforced and armored wagons that were hauling the gold from the Mint to the train depot were disguised as freight wagons —"

"Just as I guessed!" Jay interrupted.

"These gold wagons, in order to keep from attracting attention to themselves, were unescorted and, besides the driver, had only one man riding, and each guard was carrying only concealed weapons under his coat — no shot-guns."

"Pretty risky way to transport gold."

"It was only a few miles through the city. It had worked before. Anyway, the wagons left the Mint at 3:30 A.M. on Saturday morning, when the city was as quiet and deserted as it was likely to get. They'd gone only three blocks when about a dozen armed men very quietly hijacked them. The drivers and guards said they came up on foot out of the fog from behind the wagons. They were all dressed in dark clothes and wore masks — Oriental masks — and gloves. They tied up and gagged the four men on the wagons and dragged them back into an alley and put them in some trash barrels. They simply drove off with the wagons. Of course they had to have inside help, since the delivery was a closely guarded secret. Anyway, since the wagons were on a very strict schedule they were missed at the depot very shortly and a search was started. That's why I think they had to have a prearranged site where they stashed the gold — someplace fairly close, because they knew someone would come looking for the wagons quickly. The Mint is on Fifth Street and the brewery on Second Street."

"Were the wagons found?"

"Yes. About daylight. Parked only a short distance from where the drivers and guards were found. One of the guards finally knocked over the trash barrel, worked his gag loose, and yelled for help."

"So you think they unloaded the gold at Wieland's Brewery?"

"Yes. Until you showed up with your story, no one had any reason to connect the brewery with the robbery. I think one or more men at the brewery had to be involved with the robbery because no one there reported a break-in. And how else could all that gold have been unloaded and hidden inside full kegs of beer? It would have taken several men, working fast, to get that much gold moved and hidden between . . . let's say . . . about four-fifteen and whenever the brewery opened on Saturday morning."

"Normally about seven."

"And that included the time it must have taken to pry or blast open those armored wagons. Actually, the doors of the wagons showed signs of acid burns and pry bars, so I guess no explosives were used.

"They knew about you," Fred continued. "They knew you would be making a delivery to Cliff House that morning. They had the fire set at Cliff House to cause confusion so they could hijack your wagon, with you on it, and force you to drive an innocent-looking beer wagon into Chinatown in daylight."

"Maybe that's why I wasn't fired Saturday morning after my wreck. Maybe the old man, Carl Bauer, knew I had to make that run to Cliff House."

"Could be. I'm sure the old man will be questioned thoroughly."

"I wonder where the wagon is?"

"Probably dismantled and hidden in many cellars. The horses would be a little harder to hide, but they're probably out of the city by now. Anyway, you can bet the Secret Service is down at the brewery now, making a lot of inquiries. Until you escaped no one suspected the Chinese. Quite the opposite, since the robbers wore Oriental masks. So it appears now that the hijackers had made very thorough and elaborate plans and carried them out to the letter. And these plans apparently included bribing a number of whites to help them."

"That's just what Yen Ching told me."

Casey nodded. "So at this point, I'm forced to conclude that everything Yen Ching told you is true. Of course, I have no way of knowing whether his plans of getting the gold to Mexico and setting up a revolutionary headquarters are true. There's only one thing that bothers me."

"What's that?"

"Your wagon could not have held the entire three million in gold. As I said, it had to weigh more than four tons. What was the capacity of your wagon?"

Jay thought for a few seconds. "Well, I don't know. It had a really heavy-duty undercarriage. And it would hold twenty-eight barrels of beer. One of those kegs full weighs about two hundred pounds. That would be . . . around five thousand pounds, loaded to capacity. Around two and a half tons, I'd say."

"See what I mean? I doubt if your wagon could hold a load that would be twice as heavy as a full load of beer. Maybe half again as much, but not twice. And if it could, would a team of four horses be able to pull it?"

"I see what you mean. It must have been a heavier than normal load. I remember the team straining pretty hard that morning. I thought something was wrong with the wagon."

"If they loaded those kegs with a combination of coins and beer that was about equal to, or a little more than, a normal load of beer, then where did the rest of the gold go?"

Jay looked blank. "You tell me."

"I have no idea. I was just thinking out loud."

"What do you think they'll find at the brewery?"

"Nothing. The same thing we found at the Chee Kong tong headquarters. And with no evidence I'm sure no arrests will be made. The people involved in this have all been very careful up to this point."

"Wouldn't it have been a lot easier and smarter to steal paper money? Maybe a large payroll or two, or hold up a bank? Stacks of greenbacks would be a lot easier to haul around and hide than tons of gold," Jay reasoned.

"For a couple of reasons. First, greenbacks are easily traceable due to serial numbers. Secondly, gold is negotiable anywhere in the world, and presumably this is to be used on an international scale to finance a revolution."

"Do you think Lee Sing is an accomplice?"

Casey shook his head. "I believe she's just what she appears to be — an innocent victim of circumstances who used that raid as a means of escape from bondage. And because she either felt sorry for you or for some reason took a liking to you, she rescued you at the same time." Casey looked sideways at Jay and grinned, his blue eyes twinkling. "No doubt your looks and your killin' ways."

"You said it." He scrubbed a hand over his unshaven face and grinned back. "But whatever it was, I'm sure grateful to her. I might be dead by now."

"I doubt it. They could have killed you when you were first captured and brought there. They either really wanted you to guide them to Mexico or they were hesitant to kill a white man."

"Why's that?"

"The Chinese tongs have avoided big trouble in this city for years by confining their killing to each other. As long as they don't kill Caucasians there won't be a big uproar about the crime in Chinatown. And they know this. That's why the Chinese tongs have operated strictly within their own race and their own boundary."

They reached the California Street station house, and Jay lounged outside on the steps while Fred went inside to report that Lee Sing had been placed in the custody of the Methodist Mission.

"I'm officially off duty now. Let's go to my place," Fred said, coming out and bounding down the steps. "I'm sure Lee Sing will be given a few hours' rest and then she'll be brought down to the station and questioned by all the detectives and Secret Service men involved in this case. I got permission to take you into police custody for your own safety, and so you'll be available for further questioning. That's why you're going to my place."

The sun was high now and burning off the fog rapidly. Its warming rays were a welcome relief to Jay after the chill of the night.

"I probably need to go by my room and get some other clothes and my toothbrush and some things," Jay said. "I feel silly walking around in this Chinese garb."

"No. As well organized as this bunch of thieves is, they probably know where you live and have someone watching the place right now. We don't want to lose you now, since you just got away from them. You can wear some of my clothes; we're about the same size."

The clacking of the moving cable under the street could be heard as they walked along. Even though the business day had started, there was little traffic on this side street at 10:00 A.M. on a Monday morning. Was it really only Monday morning? It seemed to Jay that the events since Friday had stretched back over at least a month.

"Let's grab the cable car. It'll cut a few

blocks off our walk," Fred said, stepping off the curbing as they heard the car's bell clanging from a block away.

CHAPTER 10

Jay absolutely refused to take the only bed in his friend's boardinghouse room. But as soon as Fred had borrowed a spare mattress from the landlady and spread it on the floor in the corner, Jay was on it, wrapped in a blanket, and dead asleep in ten minutes.

Fred let him sleep the rest of the day and on into the evening. Whenever he left the house it was only for short periods to buy a newspaper, eat some lunch, pick up a razor and toothbrush at a corner store. He had the uneasy feeling he was being watched, but never saw anyone as he came and went without his uniform. He always locked the door to his room and alerted the landlady, Mrs. Peterson, to tell anyone who might come looking for him or his friend that they had gone out for the day — especially if any inquirers happened to be Oriental. That way he would also be assured of not getting the message if anyone were sent from the station house asking him to work overtime tonight on his scheduled night off.

He finally came back to his room about two o'clock in the afternoon, pulled off his clothes, and climbed wearily into bed himself.

When Jay awoke, gray light was filtering in through the drawn blinds at the bay window that faced the street. He didn't know if it was dawn or dusk. He stretched and yawned and, after a few minutes, pushed himself up off the mattress. He felt somewhat disoriented as the events of the past few days came flooding back into his mind. Maybe it had all been a dream, he reflected, as he rubbed the sleep from his eyes and pulled aside the blinds to look out. It was dusk. He must have slept the day away. He felt rested and refreshed. He didn't have a watch but guessed it must be about eight o'clock. Fred's steady breathing could be heard in the quiet room.

Just as Jay was rolling up his blanket Fred rolled over and came to full wakefulness almost immediately — a trait that had served him well on several occasions as a policeman who was on call or had to work long hours at a stretch with only time for catnaps.

"Sleep well?" he asked as he climbed out of bed.

"Great."

"Let me find some clothes for you. After you get cleaned up we'll go get some supper."

As they were going out the landlady stopped them. She was a buxom, middle-aged widow who was very careful of her dress and manners and, Fred said, just as meticulous about those of her boarders.

"A gentleman from the station house called for you earlier," she told Fred as she accosted them in the foyer. "He said to tell you that you were to report for duty at the Embarcadero at ten o'clock tonight."

"Oh no!" Casey groaned.

"He said there was a ship arriving from Canton and another one leaving with a load o' them Chinese bodies bein' sent back to China for burial. You have to be there to inspect 'em."

"Did he just ask, or was it an order?"

"Sounded to me like an order. Go along with ya, now. You're a young, strong

Irish lad, and the city needs more like ya."

She hustled them out the door.

"Her name is Mrs. Bridget Peterson, but her maiden name was O'Toole," Casey explained as they went down the sidewalk. "Straight from the auld sod. She's kinda taken to motherin' me."

"Why do you have to inspect a bunch of bodies being shipped out?" Jay asked.

"Contraband. It's not so much the bodies but the live coolies leaving. One of the Six Companies gives each of them a slip of paper which, in effect, is their clearance to leave the country. It's a statement that they have paid all their debts here and have no creditors. It's a good idea. They're not supposed to be able to purchase a ticket without that receipt from one of the Six Companies that shows they are free and clear to go. Probably be a couple o' the other boys on the force down there, too, inspectin' the incoming ship for opium and any slave girls that might be disembarking."

"How do you know a slave girl from anyone else?" Jay wanted to know.

"You don't, for sure," Casey shrugged. "But it's a pretty good guess that if a couple of dozen young females come ashore with one or two men those girls are destined for the houses of prostitution of Chinatown. Even if some of them have written agreements that they have accepted passage money to come here and work for a Chinaman, you can bet that agreement will never be honored. She'll probably be sold to the highest bidder within twenty-four hours of her arrival, for as much as three thousand dollars."

Jay gave a low whistle. "There's a tremendous demand for these so-called 'singsong' girls, then?"

Fred nodded. "A number of them are even taken into the interior of California and Nevada to the mining towns, where there are groups of Chinese working. There's such a demand right here in the city that one tong is stealing them from another. One of their favorite ploys is to hire some whites to pose as police and stage a raid on a house of joy, arrest the girls, and then turn them over to a rival tong."

"How do people like Mrs. Frierson get involved in this?"

"They're not out stealing the girls, if that's what you mean. The ladies of the Methodist and Presbyterian Missions just provide sanctuary for any girls who manage to get away. They've been doing it on a small scale since the early seventies. The girls usually stay there at the expense of the churches until they can make a better life for themselves either by getting a job, marrying, or going back to China. But even at the missions they're often not completely safe. One of the tricks their former masters pull is to file a formal complaint of theft against a girl, cause her to be arrested and brought to court where bail is set. Then the former master pays the bail and that's the last anyone sees of that poor girl, who disappears back into his employ as a prostitute in Chinatown somewhere."

"Damn! I hope Mrs. Frierson keeps a tight rein on Lee Sing, no matter who comes to the door."

"I think I impressed on her that Lee Sing is a special case."

The gas street lamps were glowing softly in the gathering darkness and Jay was turning up his coat collar at the night chill as they turned into a restaurant.

"You probably ought to stay in my room again tonight, and keep the door locked," Fred said after they had placed their order for steak and potatoes.

Jay looked startled. "I thought I was coming with you."

Fred hesitated. "Well, I guess it won't hurt anything. In fact it may be better than you staying at the boardinghouse. This way you'll be in protective custody and I can keep an eye on you. You might even find it interesting."

"Good. Will you be on duty all night, or just until they get the ships loaded and unloaded?"

"Just until I get finished, if that's before daylight. This is supposed to be my night off."

Jay nodded and sipped the scalding coffee the waiter poured for him.

"By the way, do you have a gun?" Casey asked.

"Sure. It's in my room. Why?"

"Well, the waterfront at night is not the safest place in the world. When we finish eating, give me your key and let me go by there and get it. I'm not in uniform yet. No one will pay any attention to me if some o' that tong are watching your place."

Just before ten o'clock Jay and Fred

148

arrived at the Embarcadero on the north end of the penisular city. This waterfront area was a clutter of warehouses set among a maze of wharves. Heavy drays were parked near loading platforms. The dirt underfoot would have been as hard as wooden planks had it not been for the frequent scuffing of hooves of hogs and cattle passing through this area on their way to market. Illuminated by the gaslights, and fading on into the darkness beyond the fingers of piers, was a virtual forest of tall masts and the spidery tracery of rigging. Even the big steamers with their black stacks had not given up their masts and crossed yardarms. It was wise not to rely totally on steam for ocean passages.

Fred Casey seemed very familiar with the area and went striding off in the semidarkness until he found the pier he was looking for. To Jay it looked no different than a dozen others, but Fred hailed two of his fellow officers who had already arrived.

"What're you doing here, Fred? I thought you'd be working on that big break in the Mint robbery case," a big curly-haired man greeted Casey.

Casey made a face. "No respect for genius, I suppose. Maybe the chiefs figure I was just in the right place at the right time to get the story first, because I happened to be a good friend of the man who escaped to break it to us." He turned to Jay. "And gentlemen, behold the man who was there — Jay McGraw himself." He swept his arm toward Jay as if introducing a celebrated personage.

Jay was glad they couldn't see his face reddening in the dim light.

"Have the newspaper reporters caught up with you yet?" one of the men asked.

"Reporters?"

"Sure. This is big news. You'll be on the front page tomorrow morning or I'll miss my guess."

"No. I haven't talked to any reporters."

"He's in my protective custody," Casey said.

"You'll be quoted, nonetheless."

"But I haven't talked to any newspaper people," Jay objected.

"The reporters won't let that stand in the way of a good exciting story or direct quote. What details they couldn't get from the commissioner they'll invent. I can see it now: Break in Mint

Robbery Case. Gold Seen Hidden in Chinatown. Daring Rooftop Escape by Kidnapped Deliveryman Reveals Bizarre Plot."

Jay laughed. "If they want anything directly from me, I'll have to get permission from your bosses before I talk to them."

A steam whistle bleated somewhere in the distance of the Bay, muffled by the incoming fog.

"Looks like another pea-souper," the blue-coated, curly-haired man said, squinting toward the darkness beyond the piers. "Your ship won't get up steam and out of here before the fog lifts in the morning," he said to Fred. "They'll take their time loading those bodies." He grinned. "You'll be here 'til daylight."

"Just which one *is* the *City of Peking*?" Fred asked. "It's supposed to be at Pier Eight."

"That's it right over there. The big one with the black hull. They put 'er in another slip 'cause she was so long."

"Well, here comes the gangway down. I guess we'd better get to work. See you later."

The two policemen turned away to begin checking the passengers leaving a big square-rigger.

"Do they inspect the ship for opium after the passengers come ashore?" Jay asked, shifting his holstered Colt Lightning under his coat.

"Yes, but it's usually just a formality. Most of the drug is dropped overside to a waiting lugger or rowboat out in the Bay. Sometimes they even drop it to a waiting boat outside the Golden Gate, even before the ship takes the harbor pilot aboard."

Jay's attention was distracted by the clopping of horses' hooves and the jingling of trace chains. Along the dirt street just behind the row of wharves came a slow parade of wagons stacked high with wooden rectangular boxes. Each wagon was driven by a Chinese man, each wearing a low-crowned, straight-brimmed black hat and black, loose-fitting top and trousers. They were as alike as if they had been in uniform. The somber drivers drew up, two abreast, and several Orientals swarmed down from the black-hulled depths of the *City of Peking* and began unloading the wooden coffins.

Jay looked back along the row of wagons and made a rough estimate.

"There must be at least two hundred bodies there."

"Closer to three hundred, if I'm any judge," Casey replied. "They save 'em up for months, and then ship 'em back to the old country for burial. Some are buried here, of course, in a Chinese cemetery near the city. But most of them don't want to be planted on our soil among the 'fan kwei' — the foreign devils."

"Do you have to inspect every one of them?"

Casey shook his head. "I just open a few at random. It's a hit-or-miss operation. We don't really expect to find anything. It's mostly done just to keep the Chinese aware of a police presence on the waterfront. As I mentioned, most of the contraband, in the form of girls and opium, is coming into the country, not going out."

They moved closer to the first wagon, where the driver sat, one leg thrown over the back of the seat, smoking a cigarette, as the stevedores clumped across the wooden planks of the pier and up the gangway with the wooden coffins, two men to a box.

"This is going to take a while," Jay

remarked, looking back along the row of wagons in the swirling fog that was now rolling in in earnest, nearly obscuring the rest of the waterfront in spite of the gaslights.

"It sure is." Casey stepped forward and held up his hand, then pointed for two of the crewmen to set one of the boxes off to the side on the ground. He reached under the seat of the first wagon and secured a claw hammer and crowbar that the drivers always carried, and began gently prying the lid up. The boxes were crudely made and nailed together. The top came off and they peered in. By the dim light of a nearby street lamp they saw a Chinese man in dark, quilted garments. His yellow face looked sunken and withered.

"Whew!" Fred dropped the lid and tapped the nails back into place. "They do a good job of embalming, but some o' these bodies still smell pretty rank." He took the hammer and gently rapped the sides and end of the box from the outside. "Sometimes you can tell by the sound if there's a hollow compartment."

They continued to inspect every seventh to tenth box that came along. After about two hours of this Jay was ready to pack it in, but he said nothing and kept doggedly at it. There was nothing much to be seen beyond the many bodies, some recently dead and in a better state of preservation than others. Jay hoped none of them had died of a contagious disease.

"Don't the Chinese resent this as a desecration or anything?" Jay asked finally. Not one of the Chinese laborers or drivers had spoken a word to them.

Casey shrugged as he stood up and wiped a sleeve across his damp brow. "Never gave it much thought. They just know it's required, so they don't say anything. If there's any protest made, it's done at a higher level."

By three-thirty in the morning, they were nearly finished.

"Now all we have to do is examine the papers of the passengers to see if they've got their debt-free receipts from one of the Six Companies." He gestured at the small groups of men who were sitting on valises and talking nearby.

When Jay and Fred finally walked away from the docks, the gray light of another day was pearling the chilly fog. About two blocks away they caught a cable car, and Jay sank down gratefully

155

in the seat. They were the only passengers. They were both tired. And they had found nothing out of the ordinary. Just another routine night shift for Fred Casey, a member of the special Chinatown Squad. Police work could be as dull as anything else, Jay reflected.

As the cable car clacked and clanged its way along, Jay wondered idly what this day would bring. There had certainly been nothing routine about his life the past few days.

CHAPTER 11

Although Jay had no way of knowing it, two related events were occurring that day which would predict his destiny.

But for the moment the only thought on his mind was breakfast and bed, in that order, with possibly a good hot bath in between.

After they had eaten Fred offered to accompany Jay to see his boss at Wieland's Brewery. They rode a cable car to within two blocks and walked the rest of the way.

"Hey, McGraw!" the loading dock foreman hailed him, stepping out into the early morning sunshine. He glanced curiously at Casey's blue uniform and badge. "Been readin' about you in the *Chronicle.* That's one helluva tale. This place has been crawlin' with police and all kinds of officials since yesterday."

"Morning, Jake. Is old man Bauer in?"

"Yeah. He's in the office." He jerked his

head in the general direction. "Say, is that story about you really true? Did you really get kidnapped and all that?" He looked incredulous.

The meeting with Carl Bauer was brief. The old man, baggy eyes testifying to a sleepless night, regretted that he could not keep Jay on as an employee, but the loss of a valuable wagon and team, not to mention a load of beer, could not be tolerated. In his heavy accent he explained, glancing at Casey, that the brewery had also been getting a lot of bad publicity due to the robbery at the Mint. All undeserved, of course. If, for some unexplained reason, stolen gold had been found in some of Wieland's barrels, it was certainly not the fault of the company that some robbers had taken advantage of the company to do this evil thing, and so forth. Listening to him, Jay felt that his firing would have been a lot briefer and blunter, with maybe some hints at Jay's own possible involvement, had not Fred Casey, representing the law, been standing there.

Jay was relieved when he left the old man and went by the paymaster's window to pick up his final week's pay. A few minutes later, after saying quick good-byes to several friends he had made at the brewery and promising to come back and visit them if he got the chance, he and Casey left to go to the boardinghouse.

"Several of those people asked if I was under arrest when they saw you," Jay said when they were back out on the sidewalk.

"Don't mind that," Casey said. "You know that you weren't involved, and that's all that matters."

As they walked up Second Street, Jay hailed a boy in knickers who was hawking the morning newspaper and bought a copy. As they rode the cable car, he and Casey perused the stories that were front-page news about the big break in the robbery. In their haste to get to print the reporters had garbled many of the facts. One of the editorials on an inside page even hinted that Jay had made up the whole thing and that somehow he had masterminded the plot. Another speculated that he was a publicity-seeker who actually had had nothing whatever to do with the robbery.

Jay finally folded up the paper and yawned mightily. "I tell you what, this high adventure is exhausting."

They returned to Casey's boarding-house and both slept the day away, after telling Mrs. Peterson that they were not to be disturbed except for an emergency. Jay went to sleep comforted by the thought that his own room rent was paid up for the next two weeks in advance and that he had a little money in his pocket from his last wages, so that he wouldn't have to be entirely dependent on his friend until he could find other work. He hoped the publicity he was getting wouldn't prevent someone from hiring him because they thought he was unreliable or dishonest.

"Hell, if nothing else, you can go on a lecture tour with a hair-raising tale of your adventures," Casey said when Jay mentioned this. Although it was said in jest, Jay realized that other careers had been built on just such beginnings.

Two days passed — two days in which Jay became increasingly restless. At Fred Casey's insistence he remained at Casey's boardinghouse, and indoors during the night hours when Casey was on duty patrolling the streets of China-town. For a good part of each day he sat in various offices, being repeatedly questioned by different police and Secret Service men. They wrung out his memory for every half-remembered detail of his kidnapping and escape. After a few hours of this Jay felt he could now probably repeat verbatim his conversation with the tong chief Yen Ching.

"Lord, I hope this is finished soon," Jay complained to Fred the second evening, as they sat at supper in a small restaurant. "I want to go looking for a job and get back to living a normal life."

Fred nodded and spoke around a mouthful of fresh bread. "They're pretty well stumped, and I think all this questioning is just so they might bring out some detail that may not seem important to you but may be valuable to them. They're looking for anything, however small, that might put them on the trail again."

"Are they doing the same thing to Lee Sing?"

"Yes. If anything, they're grilling her even harder."

"I wonder if they think she had something to do with it?"

Fred shrugged. "Anything's possible. For all we know, she may have been ordered to help you escape so you could tell your story — a story Yen Ching wanted us to hear because it would lead us on a false trail."

Jay stared at him with the fork partway to his mouth. "Do you really think that's what happened?"

"I don't know. I'm just speculating. You've already found out yourself how devious the Chinese mind can be."

"There would have been no reason to let me go at all, because no one suspected any Chinese of that robbery in the beginning, did they?"

"Not as far as I know. The Secret Service and our city detectives don't really confide in me."

"Besides," Jay said, resuming his eating, "you wouldn't even suggest that if you had seen the way Lee Sing looked at me."

"I believe you really like that girl. You'd best be thinking with your head and not your heart."

"It's not just that. I think she helped me escape because she felt she could trust me to protect her once she got away from them."

"I think by the end of the week you can probably go back to living your own life, when things begin to calm down."

"I can hardly wait."

"Still, I think we need to stay in close contact. And don't leave the city."

"Why? So I can be available for more questioning?"

"Yes. But more so because I believe you'll be safe as long as you're here. As I said before, the Chinese have avoided serious trouble from white law by confining their criminal activities to other Chinese. As far as I know there is no record of them murdering a white man in San Francisco. Maybe a few have been killed in self-defense over the years, but no murder."

"That's comforting."

"Of course they could just make you disappear some foggy night."

"But why?"

"From what you told me about your initiation into the Chee Kong tong, you swore to help your brother tong members and never betray the tong's cause or your blood would pollute the soil, and no matter where you went the tong would find you."

Jay nodded.

"Well, all that mumbo jumbo might have been staged for your benefit. But on the other hand it might have been serious. If it's serious, they could be sending a highbinder to take care of the traitorous white dog in the traditional Chinese tong method."

"And that is?"

"Cleaving your skull with a hatchet."

Jack sat back and pushed his plate away. "Suddenly I don't feel hungry anymore."

The next day Jay visited Lee Sing at the Methodist Mission. They sat in the parlor and talked for a while. Lee indicated that she was comfortable and all her needs were provided for. She said the ladies had been very nice to her and would hardly let her do any of the work. She told him that another Chinese girl who had run away from one of the houses on Clay Street had been brought to the mission, so she had had someone of her own race to talk to for a day. But then the girl had been offered, and taken, a chance to be sent home to China to her family. Lee Sing expressed a desire to be able to leave the mission as well, and Jay assured her that she would be free to go as soon as the police had finished questioning her and were convinced she would be safe.

When Jay left after an hour or so he had the distinct feeling that he did not know Lee Sing at all. He sensed a reserved quality about her. Even though on the surface she was as friendly as she had ever been, he got the feeling she was nervous and preoccupied about something. Maybe it was there all along and I was just too busy to notice, Jay thought as he walked up the street in the brilliant sunshine.

He had gotten into the habit, the past few days, of carrying his Colt Lightning in a small holster on his left hip under his coat whenever he went out. He was also more aware of who was around him on the street. He was constantly alert to anyone who looked to be Oriental. He wanted no surprises.

But a surprise he got. It came that very night, just as he and Fred Casey were going out to a late supper around nine o'clock. A patrolman from Fred's own station house came rushing up to them just as they were coming down the steps from the boardinghouse.

"Fred! They got the girl!"

"What?"

"They got the girl. Lee Sing. The tong took her from the mission."

"Dammit!" Casey ground his teeth in frustration. "How?"

"One of their tricks. Mrs. Frierson is beside herself. They apparently hired a white man to dress up like a police officer and go to the door and tell Mrs. Frierson that Lee Sing was wanted at the station house for more questioning. Mrs. Frierson was suspicious when she didn't recognize the officer and asked why she was being summoned at the dinner hour. He told her there'd been some new developments in the case and she was needed right away. So she finally let Lee Sing go with him. But she watched as they went down the street. And suddenly two highbinders jumped out of a closed carriage at the curb and grabbed her. The 'policeman' got in with them and they took off in the direction of Chinatown."

"Oh no!" Jay felt as if someone had kicked him in the stomach. He had promised to protect this girl, who had befriended him and helped him escape, and now he had let her fall back into the hands of the tong. He should have taken her out of the mission sooner, but there would have been no place for her to go. Maybe she could have been boarded at the police station house. Surely they couldn't have gotten her there. That was probably why she had seemed so nervous this morning.

But regrets were useless and he brought his attention back to the matter at hand, as Fred was questioning the patrolman for more details about what had happened and the time of the incident.

"Well, there's nothing that can be done about it now," he concluded, shaking his head. "You can bet they've got her someplace where we'll never find her. It would be like trying to find a particular fish in the Bay."

"You're not even going to try?" Jay asked.

"Oh, we'll try. I'm sure the captain has some men out right now. And I'll do what I can when I'm on patrol there tonight. But I can tell you right now, it's useless."

They discussed the incident over supper but got no further than before. Then Jay went back to the room and tried to lose himself in sleep. It was difficult. He tossed and turned and dozed. Finally, in the early hours of the morning, he slept fitfully and dreamed of Chinese hatchet men chasing him in the streets. His legs were so heavy he couldn't run. When he tried to draw his gun the hammer snagged in his coattail, just as a grinning yellow face bore down on him, an arm swinging a shiny meat cleaver.

He awoke in a sweat, gasping, but grateful that it was just a nightmare. He got up and paced the floor, looking out the window at the gray dawn creeping over the city. By the time Fred came in from his night shift Jay was composed, dressed, and waiting for him to go to get some morning coffee.

"Any news of Lee Sing?" Jay asked as they started out to breakfast.

"Nope. Ever since the two of you showed up at the station house that morning there's been a force of plain clothes detectives scouring Chinatown. And they're thinking now that both the gold and the girl have been taken out of the city somewhere. Chinese people are very conspicuous. It's not as if they could just blend into the population anywhere in California, especially Chinese people with at least two freight wagons of gold. They're thinking now that the gold may have been smuggled out of Chinatown a little at a time, hidden in a thousand different places."

"They don't believe that Yen Ching is trying to get it all to Mexico, then?"

"That's one of the theories they're looking at. The Mexican authorities have been alerted, but there are many miles of border between this country and Mexico that cannot be patrolled. One could cross 'most anywhere and not be seen.

"By the way, the captain was asking me if you might be interested in working for the police force, if you're looking for a job."

"What? Me?"

"Yes. For some reason, he's taken a liking to you. Thinks you're a very resourceful young man and have a head on your shoulders. And frankly the force is shorthanded, what with our regular duties and all this overtime because of the robbery. We didn't have that many men to start with."

"I can't imagine myself wearing a uniform."

"Well, you wouldn't be in uniform. He's not authorized to hire uniformed police on his own. But there is some extra money he can use at his own discretion in unusual situations such as this, to hire extra temporary help. You'd be issued a badge and sworn in.

You'd be something like a special detective."

Jay laughed as they sat down in their favorite restaurant to order toast and coffee.

"Are you interested?"

"Sure. But I'd have no idea what I'm to do."

"Don't worry. They'll instruct you. In fact, there's a good possibility that you'd be sent out to the interior of the state to check some of the mining towns, and maybe follow up on any reports of movements of Chinese who are not residents of some of those small towns."

Jay shrugged. "Beats sitting in your room all day with nothing to do. Sure, I'll do it."

"Good. We'll go back by the station house right after breakfast and get you sworn in."

Fred was as good as his word and, just over an hour later, Jay McGraw was officially a member of the San Francisco Police Force, Detective Division. Since he already had his own side arm, he was authorized to carry that when on official police business.

"Besides detectives, is there anyone else in plain clothes?" Jay asked as they left the station house.

"There are Secret Service men and Wells Fargo detectives as well, but I don't know how many altogether. They're spread out all over the place, and I don't know most of them."

About mid-afternoon there was a knock at Fred Casey's boardinghouse door. Fred was asleep and Jay was sitting near an open window, reading a book. Jay jumped and yanked his Colt. He went to the door and put his hand on the bolt. "Who is it?"

"Mrs. Peterson. There's a lad here from the station house with a message for Fred Casey."

Jay slid back the bolt and opened the door, slipping his Colt out of sight as he did so. A boy of about fourteen stood there, cap in hand, holding an envelope. Jay took it. "Thank you. I'll see that he gets it. He's asleep just now."

"He must read it now, sir. It's very urgent."

Jay glanced at Mrs. Peterson, who stood behind the boy, but her face was impassive.

"Do you need to wait for an answer?"

The boy shook his head. "No, but I was

to tell Mr. Casey that he is to report to the station house right away."

Jay tipped the messenger with a silver twenty-five-cent piece and closed the door. Then he woke Fred and handed him the envelope, relaying the boy's verbal instructions. Fred sat up, rubbing sleep from his eyes, and tore open the missive, holding it to the afternoon light from the window.

He read the message through and then broke into a slow smile. "Well, it looks as if you and I will be taking a little trip together."

"Where?"

"Down the coast to Los Angeles, to begin with. A man who looks like Yen Ching has been spotted there. He's being watched by Secret Service agents, but he can't be arrested because he hasn't done anything. Since you're the only one who can identify him positively, the captain wants you to go down and take a look. I'm to accompany you and give you some pointers in police work as we go, now that you're a duly sworn-in detective."

"Isn't this a little unusual?" Jay asked as Fred was pulling on his clothes.

"Yes it is. But this is an unusual case,

and they're grabbing at any lead they can get, using any method necessary. We'd better get down to the station house. They want us on the seven o'clock train."

CHAPTER 12

"Nice of the city to pay for a sleeping car," Fred remarked as they rattled south on the rails at nine that night. "But I was ready to work all night, so I'm not even sleepy. I'll have to get my days and nights turned back around again."

Jay sat reading the newspaper under the lamp in the gently rocking car. "Here's some more speculation about the robbery."

"What's it say?"

"Just mentions that the authorities think the gold was taken out of the city. Tells about Lee Sing's kidnapping. And it even mentions my name. Says I'm being sent to Los Angeles."

"What?"

"Yeah. Here it is. Take a look."

Fred Casey leaned over to scan the column. He frowned. "Wonder how they found out about that? Normally, no details of the investigation are published

174

— especially when it involves the movement of detectives. I'm surprised it's in the paper. I'll bet the captain's mad as hell about that — if he's seen it. Maybe you were singled out because of your sudden fame in this case."

They discussed the case some more, then Fred got out a deck of cards and played some solitaire. In spite of his claim that he was not tired he was in his berth by midnight, an hour after Jay had retired to his.

They were met the next evening at the Los Angeles depot by a young man in his early thirties wearing a dark gray suit, white shirt and tie, and a black hat. He was clean-shaven, had thinning, light brown hair, and was of medium build.

"Glen Bassett," the man said, extending his hand. "I was told to meet you."

"You're with the government?"

Bassett nodded. "Treasury Department."

"How'd you know who we were?" Casey asked as they let the crowd of debarking passengers swirl past them. The black locomotive stood panting and steaming at the end of the platform.

"Recognized you from the good de-

scriptions I got. Here, let me get those."
Jay noted the pistol strapped under the
man's coat as he leaned over to take the
leather grips.

They walked off down the depot platform.

"I think that's a good idea, you coming
down here," Bassett said.

"Well, if I can help identify Yen Ching,
I'll do it," Jay replied.

"Well, yeah, that too," Glen Bassett
said, glancing curiously at Jay.

"What do you mean?" Fred asked.

"I mean it takes a lot of guts, after
what you've already been through, to
set yourself up as a decoy," Bassett
replied.

"A decoy?"

"They didn't tell you, did they?" Bassett stopped walking and turned to face
them. "You are being put on public dis-
play, so to speak, so the hatchet men of
the Chee Kong tong will come after you.
If they do, the law will be watching and
give us a chance to grab them and get a
lead on the gold. That's as blunt as I can
put it."

He started walking again. "I'm sorry
you didn't know. But I think it's unfair
they didn't tell you. If a man is risking

his life, I think he should at least know about it."

Fred Casey's fair face was beginning to redden as this information sank in. "Those sneaky bastards!" he grated under his breath. "Both of us could have been killed on that train and never known what hit us. That's the reason Jay's name and destination were in the *Chronicle*."

"I hope both of you are armed," Bassett said.

"We are."

"Good. Keep alert to everyone on the street. There aren't as many Chinese in this city, so you might tend to get a little careless."

"Not after what you just told us."

"Don't just look at the clothing. Some of these hatchet men could be dressed in normal western clothing. It would be best to stay out of crowds and public places."

"Don't worry about that," Jay answered, glancing around at the thinning crowd as they walked through the waiting room.

"I got you a room at the Claremore Hotel. You're on the second floor just above the lobby, window facing the front of the building, empty rooms reserved on each side of you being watched by our men. We'll have your meals brought to your room."

Jay had never thought of himself as being in real danger, even when Fred insisted that he come and stay in his boardinghouse. But the way this agent was talking he was beginning to get a little paranoid. Maybe he had a right to start getting nervous. Apparently, the authorities believed his story. He wiped a sleeve across his clammy brow. He was sweating, but it wasn't from fear. It was just hot here. Or at least a lot warmer than in San Francisco.

Bassett hailed a cab waiting at the curb, put their bags in the back, and the three of them climbed in. The rig was a lightweight, high-wheeled wagon with a canopy over the top and three bench seats facing forward. The driver clucked to the horse and they moved off toward downtown.

"Where is this man who looks like Yen Ching?" Jay asked.

"We have two men keeping an eye on him. He's staying at a place a few blocks from the waterfront. As soon as you get settled in I'll take you down there. We've still got about three hours of daylight. He generally stays in this small house where there are two other Chinese living, but he goes in about sunset and doesn't come back out until the next day."

"If it's the same man I met I'm surprised he can even walk," Jay said. "He was huge."

"This man is, too. He doesn't walk far. Usually has a rig waiting for him at the door."

"Where does he go? What does he do during the day?" Fred Casey asked.

"He stays pretty much within the small Chinese community here. I don't know whether it's business or he's visiting friends or relatives. Our men have been careful not to let anyone know they're tailing him. He must be here on some sort of business because he's visited a warehouse and also the Southern Pacific freight office."

As soon as they had checked into their hotel, Bassett hired a hack and they headed for the waterfront. When they neared the neighborhood they got out, paid the driver, and walked the last three blocks. Most of the buildings here were one-story, flat-roofed adobes, mixed in with a few frame houses with the paint peeling. Some Mexican children were running and playing in the dusty yards of a few of the houses. The smell of cooking onions made Jay's stomach growl.

Bassett led them to the back of an empty shed and rapped quietly. The door was opened and a red-faced man greeted them. His collar was open and he was sweating.

The three of them stepped inside to a dim light and a musty odor. The low, westerly sun slanted through the cracks in the unpainted boards. Jay noted the few downy feathers lying around and guessed they were in an unused chicken coop.

"Charlie Foss, this is Jay McGraw and Fred Casey," Glen Bassett introduced them. The beefy, red-faced Foss shook their hands. "Welcome to my humble digs."

"Where is he, Charlie?" Bassett asked. "I want McGraw to get a look at him before dark."

"He went out about noon and hasn't come back yet." Foss walked to the other side of the shed and pulled back a loose board, opening a crack about eight inches wide. Jay and Fred crowded close as he pointed across the dirt street to a flat-roofed building. "That's where he's staying. There's a bunch o' Chinese living on that next block or two."

There was nothing distinctive about the place. It was in a very poor section of town, and Jay couldn't imagine the man he knew as Yen Ching, with his mighty opinion of himself, opulent dress and surroundings, staying in a place like that. It had to be some look-alike — some poor, fat Chinaman someone had, from Jay's description, mistaken for Yen Ching. This whole thing is probably just a ruse to get me out of San Francisco so the highbinders can have a shot at me, Jay thought, turning away from the opening. He glanced around at the interior of the shed. A quilt and a few empty food cans were piled in one corner. Cigarette butts littered the dirt floor. Evidently, they *had* been using this place as a lookout post for a few days.

"Is Mel coming back to relieve you tonight?" Bassett asked Foss.

"Yeah. He should be here about nine o'clock."

"Let's wait," Bassett said. "This Chinaman usually comes in before dark. Maybe you can get a look at him."

They found themselves places on the floor and chatted in low voices as they whiled away the time. The light grew dimmer as the sun went down. Foss sat on an upturned box next to the crack and kept a constant vigil. Finally it was too dark to see anything.

"We'll try it again in the morning, Charlie," Bassett said, getting up and brushing himself off.

"I don't know what happened to him," Foss replied. "The fat man must be spending the night away. He's never this late."

"Any wife or girlfriend that you know of?" Casey asked.

"Haven't seen any women at all."

"Well, I could have tailed him today, except for meeting the train. I'll see you in the morning," Bassett said as he held the door of the shed open for Jay and Fred.

They slipped out into the cool freshness of the starlit night.

Daylight was just beginning to filter through the curtained windows of Room 202 in the Claremore Hotel when the thumping of a fist on the door startled Jay awake.

"Who is it?"

"Bassett."

The knocking and the voice sounded urgent, so Jay vaulted out of bed and had the door unlocked and open in a matter of seconds.

Bassett entered followed closely by Foss, whose red face was already perspiring.

"What's up?" Fred was already out of bed and pulling on his pants.

"The fat Chinaman is gone."

"Where?"

"Gone east on the train. Caught the Southern Pacific about midnight. Damn! We should never have let him out of our sight. I'm going to catch hell from my bosses for this. But the man had been so predictable for the past week . . ."

"How do you know where he went?" Fred asked.

"When he didn't come back last night Foss here, and Mel, another one of our operatives, went checking all the places we'd seen him go before. Finally discovered about an hour ago that he'd bought a ticket and left on the midnight train with two other Chinese men and a woman."

"A woman?" Jay arched his eyebrows. "What did she look like?"

"We never saw her; the ticket agent told us. He just said she was a young Oriental woman."

"Lee Sing?" Fred asked, looking at Jay.

Jay shook his head. "Who knows? We don't even know if this really *was* Yen Ching. The two men with him could have been his bodyguards, though."

"Where were they headed?" Fred asked, buttoning his shirt.

"The ticket agent said they bought tickets, one-way, to Tucson," Foss replied.

"Think we ought to go chasing after him?" Jay asked. "We're not even sure he's the right man."

"Yes. You're the only one who can identify him," Casey said. "And until you do, we can't wire ahead and have him arrested."

"If it *is* Yen Ching, he could be trying to decoy us away from the gold," Bassett offered, swinging a leg over a straight chair and sitting down to rest his crossed arms on the back of it.

"It's about the only lead we have,"

Casey said. "We have to follow up on it, unless you have a better idea."

Bassett shook his head. "No, I don't. It just seems like such a waste of time to go chasing some fat Chinese merchant who's only bringing in a shipment of mining machinery."

"Mining machinery?"

"Yeah. Remember I told you he spent some time at a warehouse and at the freight offices of the Southern Pacific?"

"Yes."

"Well, we made some official inquiries and found out he was arranging additional express cars to ship some hundred and fifty cases of mining machinery he had brought in on the *City of Peking*."

Jay and Fred looked slowly at each other. Their eyes locked and, almost as one, they repeated, "The *City of Peking*?"

"Yeah. The big steamship. You know it?"

Fred nodded. "Jay and I, only a few nights ago, checked a load of two to three hundred coffins that were loaded aboard that ship in San Francisco. They were Chinese bodies bound for burial in China. What is that ship doing here?"

"Are you sure it's the same vessel? Maybe there are two with the same name. Not likely, but possible."

"A big four-master, black hull and two stacks amidships?"

"That's the one."

Fred Casey sat down on the bed and stared at the far wall, his face going paler than even his normal fair complexion. "I'm getting the strangest feeling that those coffins contained more than bodies, and the crates that came off that ship here contain more than mining machinery."

"The gold!" Jay said.

Casey nodded.

There was silence in the room for several seconds.

"It fits with what Yen Ching told me about getting the gold to Mexico," Jay finally said.

"And the department is pretty sure the gold had somehow been smuggled out of Chinatown," Fred added. "I have a feeling they smuggled it out literally under our noses. It was hidden in the clothing and under those bodies. I didn't find any secret compartments because there were none. They knew we probably wouldn't touch the bodies. But if we had only lifted those coffins: the gold would have made each one maybe . . . thirty to forty pounds heavier than normal."

"What time does the next train leave?"

"I'm way ahead of you," Glen Bassett said. "I've already bought three tickets on the noon train for Tucson. You can reimburse me out of your travel expense money later."

CHAPTER 13

"This sure isn't the express," Fred remarked as their day coach ground to a halt with a squeal of brakes. "Where are we now?"

Jay shook his head. "I'm not familiar with southern California. This has to be at least the tenth stop we've made since we left the City of the Angels." Glen Bassett sat across the aisle, his hat over his face, asleep. Jay grinned as he got up and stepped out into the aisle to stretch his legs. He groaned and yawned. The grimy windows of the coach were closed against the dust and the ash and cinders from the locomotive. The afternoon was hot and stuffy.

"Hell, at this rate we'll never catch up with them."

"Relax and enjoy the trip, Fred. We'll probably find out he's a legitimate Chinese merchant. But it'll be a nice trip at the expense of the police department."

"I've learned in police work never to get too relaxed and off guard, even if you feel you're on a false trail. And I don't think this is a false trail."

The day coach was about a third full, as most of the passengers had been debarking at the numerous stops south and east of Los Angeles. The local was gradually working its way into the interior of the southern California desert.

"Dust or no dust, I've got to get some air," Fred grunted, forcing up the window beside his seat.

A few minutes later the train started with a lurch, waking Bassett who stood up, red-eyed, to get the kinks out. He had shed his suit coat and tie and looked as hot and miserable as his two companions. He combed his fingers through his disheveled hair. "And to think that some of my luckier co-workers have the job of guarding the President. They live in the capitol, keep regular hours."

"Think what a hero you'll be if you crack this case," Casey reminded him, half grinning. "This is probably the biggest robbery in the history of the country, and it involves funds from the U.S. Mint."

"I guess you're right. All the glamour and adventure of the chase, huh?" He managed a grin. "If I hadn't been up most of the night, this whole thing would look a lot better."

"Well, there's no doubt in my mind that the man we're chasing *is* Yen Ching," Jay said.

"We don't have a man in Tucson, but I telegraphed ahead to the Pima County sheriff there to arrest a very fat Chinese passenger on suspicion of robbery when he gets off the Southern Pacific express from Los Angeles, along with anyone else who happens to be with him," Bassett said. "And I told him to impound that shipment of mining machinery," he added.

"Did you tell him why?" Fred asked.

"No. Only that it was urgent, and that the U.S. Government was involved, and that the Chinaman was to be held on suspicion of robbery until we got there."

"Good thinking," Fred nodded. "It'll keep a lot of treasure hunters from bustin' into those coffins before we get there. Yen Ching must have paid a good price to have a couple of extra express cars added to that train to load all those crates."

"I'd say he can probably afford it," Jay said, wryly. "But I am surprised they would add a couple of extra cars of freight to a passenger express. Must've crossed somebody's palm."

"If he did, it was with greenbacks I'll bet, and not with double eagles. Even though the gold isn't traceable, he has to be careful he doesn't throw much of it around in one place or he'll arouse suspicion. If he was smart he probably bought a few thousand in paper money at various banks."

It was full dark by the time the train dropped the last of the small towns behind and began rolling eastward across the desert toward the Arizona border. Jay had a strange feeling as he smelled the dry desert air blowing in the open windows. The smell took him back to the nearly two years he had spent in the Arizona Territory before moving on to San Francisco. The aroma of the sage brought back recent memories of hard work and hardship, even of danger and pain. He had been falsely accused of shooting a Mexican boy in the small mining town of Washington Camp, near the Mexican border. He had escaped jail, later saved the daughter of a rancher from the Apaches, and then worked for the rancher, breaking wild mustangs. He had been pursued to Tombstone by a vengeful deputy. Other adventures had followed: The rancher, Clyde McPherson, had been involved in a shootout with some of the Clanton Gang over some stolen cattle infected with foot-and-mouth disease, and McPherson had been killed.

Fred and Glen were dozing fitfully on their upholstered seats as the car swayed and clicked rhythmically over the rails. Jay stared out the window beside his seat at the three-quarter moon silvering the still, empty desert landscape. He thought of the beautiful Karen McPherson. He had stayed on to work for her for several months after her father was killed. He and two other hands: a middle-aged, freed slave and a young Mexican American cowboy. All of the rancher's cattle had been destroyed to prevent the spread of the dreaded aftosa — foot-and-mouth disease. It had been brought across the border in the herd the Clantons had stolen and sold to McPherson. Karen McPherson had lost everything except the small ranch in the Patagonia Hills that she inherited free and clear. For only room and board he and the two other faithful hands had worked for the willful young woman. Jay had fallen hopelessly in love with her, but she had other plans. She had more living to do before she settled down to marriage, she told him one evening. So she had sold the ranch, split the profit among the four of them, and gone back to Tennessee to finish her schooling. Jay had been stricken at her leaving, but her mind was made up. She was very fond of Jay, but she did not love him and was not one to string him along. The Arizona Territory was still a little too wild for her, she told him. She still hadn't really recovered from her capture by the Apaches. She still had nightmares about it. And her own mother had been captured by them several years earlier and was never seen again. Even the whites in the region were constantly killing each other, she pointed out. The Earp and Clanton factions had had a big shootout in Tombstone in October. She was going to where things were more civilized.

When the time came, Jay had driven her in a buckboard with her luggage to Tucson and seen her off on the train.

She had hugged him on the station platform, and her gray eyes had misted over. But leave she did. Then he had taken the ranch buckboard she had given him and headed for San Francisco to experience new worlds and to get Karen McPherson out of his mind. But now he was returning to the southern Arizona Territory, and all the thoughts and feelings he believed he had put behind him came flooding back. Karen McPherson was no longer there, but all the familiar places would remind him of her — just as the sight of Chinatown would forever after remind him of Lee Sing. And what of Lee Sing? What had happened to her? He felt fairly certain she was somewhere up ahead of him in the night, headed for Tucson as the personal slave of Yen Ching. It had to be Yen Ching they were following. How did the tong leader think that he could travel inconspicuously through the country with all that gold — and as grossly obese as he was, not to mention being an Oriental? He had to attract attention somewhere. Yet only by the merest chance had he been spotted in Los Angeles. Even then he probably would have been dismissed as a merchant, except for the mention of the *City of Peking* unloading his "mining machinery" in coffin-size crates.

Jay took one last look out the window at the desert chaparral moving slowly past the train. The quiet, moonlit landscape was a balm to his nerves. He took another deep breath of air and settled himself as best he could across the double seat for some sleep. He had a feeling he was going to need it, although he fervently hoped Yen Ching and the gold would both be in the custody of the law by the time they reached Tucson. And Lee Sing . . . What of Lee Sing?

The train crossed the bridge over the Colorado River and stopped at Yuma without Jay waking up. It wasn't until they ground to a halt at Gila Bend that he roused up, nursing a crick in his neck. Here they made a thirty-minute stop for breakfast and for the locomotive to take on water. The food in the depot restaurant wasn't much, but it was cheaper than what was served in the dining car and the coffee was hot and strong. And their traveling expenses were limited. Only a few passengers from the train were in the restaurant, and by the time they were served and had eaten the conductor was yelling, *"Boooaarrrd!"*

Jay climbed up the steps to the coach, feeling revived with some food inside him. But five more slow-moving hours passed before they pulled into the depot at Tucson.

"Going on noon," Bassett grunted, pocketing his silver watch as they retrieved their leather grips from under the seats and prepared to get off.

Their boots clanked on the iron steps as they stepped down from the end platform of the coach to the wooden walkway. Jay glanced around in the brilliant sunshine. Quite a number of passengers were terminating their trip here, and even more were preparing to board. The three of them walked into the shade of the overhanging depot roof. It has to be close to ninety degrees here, Jay thought, and it's only late April. He was beginning to sweat.

"Wonder if anyone is supposed to meet us?" Bassett said.

They saw only the milling passengers and the baggage handlers trundling luggage and freight on iron-wheeled carts.

A lean man in a leather vest and drooping mustache lounged toward them. "You fellas the ones who wired me from Los Angeles?" he asked cautiously, eyeing them.

"I did," Bassett answered, glancing at the badge pinned to the man's vest and extending his hand. "Glen Bassett, U.S. Secret Service."

"I'm Tom Reeves, sheriff here." He shook hands.

Bassett slipped out a leather folder from inside the coat draped over his other arm and showed his identification, then motioned toward his companions. "This is Jay McGraw and Fred Casey with the San Francisco Police Department."

Reeves nodded solemnly at them.

"Did you arrest the Chinaman?" Bassett asked, glancing around as if he expected to see someone with him.

"There wasn't nobody by that description on the express," Reeves replied. "Fact is, there weren't no Chinamen on that train at all. There weren't anythin' much in the baggage cars, neither. At least nothing like the crates you described, marked 'mining machinery.' "

"Where could they have gone?"

"Well, I'm fixin' to tell ya. After my men had searched that train from engine to caboose and didn't find nothing, I got to questioning the conductor and it seems like the Chinaman and his friends got off at Yuma when they made a stop there. Also dropped off the extra freight cars that were carrying their boxes of machinery."

"Oh no! We went right past them in the night!" Jay groaned.

"When's the next train west?" Fred asked.

"Late tonight, I think. Better ask the ticket agent." Tom Reeves eyed them from under his hat brim. "I sent a telegraph message to Los Angeles as soon as I discovered nobody was on the express, but I guess you'd already gone. What's so important about this Chinaman, anyway?"

"Sheriff, have you got a place where we can talk?" Bassett asked, wiping the sweat from his brow.

Later the three of them sat in the sheriff's office relating their story. Reeves looked from one to the other of them as the tale unfolded. When they'd finished he whistled softly. " 'Course I read about that robbery, but I never made any connection with this."

"We need to send a telegram to the authorities at Yuma," Fred Casey said, declining a cigar the sheriff offered.

He pushed a pad and pencil toward Casey. "Write it out and it'll be on its way in a few minutes. The Western Union office is just down the street."

While Casey wrote out the message Bassett asked, "There's no faster way to get back to Yuma except wait for the next train?"

Tom Reeves shook his head. "Even if you rented horses you couldn't get there any quicker and you'd kill yourselves and the animals doing it. You'd have to have several remounts to make any time at all. There's a lot of desert between here and there — mean desert, as I guess you noticed coming down. There are some stages, but they don't run through anymore since the trains came."

Bassett pondered a moment. "I guess you're right. The next train doesn't get here until two o'clock in the morning. By the time we get back to Yuma, Yen Ching will have at least a two-day head start on us, or a little more, wherever he's headed."

"But it will take them some time to move about four tons of gold," Jay reminded him.

"Four *tons!*" the sheriff marveled.

"That's about what it weighs," Bassett said absently. "Three million dollars in new double eagles."

"Damn! I can't even imagine that. You should be able to nab him pretty quick, if he's toting all that around," Reeves said.

"I doubt it," Casey replied, looking up from the telegraph message he was composing. "This is one Oriental who plans very carefully. Nothing is left to chance."

The message was finished and a deputy was dispatched to the Western Union office with it.

"I hope you told the sheriff at Yuma that this man is dangerous, and to take precautions."

Casey nodded. "I also told him to telegraph us back here at your office as soon as he could. I told him we were coming by the next train, but couldn't get there until about one o'clock tomorrow afternoon."

"Yeah. It's about two hundred and eighty miles from here."

"Where's the nearest barbershop?"

Bassett asked. "I could use a shave and maybe a bath, too, if they've got a tub."

"There's one about three blocks from here that'll fix you right up," Sheriff Reeves said, standing up. "You boys look a little beat. Where can I find you if an answer comes to your telegraph message?"

"We'll take turns staying here. You won't have to find us," Jay said, speaking for all of them.

Casey offered to wait if the other two wanted to head for the barbershop.

As Jay stepped out into the street and squinted up into the midday sunshine at the cool Santa Catalina Mountains bulwarking the dusty adobe and clapboard town, he suddenly felt a twinge of loneliness for Karen McPherson. This was the last place he had seen her. He had put her on the train at the very depot where they had arrived and then had turned his buckboard and team westward across the desert. But it had been the balmy, mild climate of a midwinter desert — not the desert of the present that was beginning to heat up with the coming of summer.

CHAPTER 14

When the train finally began to slow as it approached the Yuma station, Jay felt as if he had been on a daycoach forever. Even though the westbound train had not been crowded, he had been able to sleep only fitfully on the double seats. After sunup he had taken to pacing through the train and standing on the end platforms of the cars, letting the fresh air whip past him and gazing at the sparse vegetation of the desert terrain.

But at last Yuma was just ahead, bared to the mercy of the sun, flat adobe buildings squatting on the Colorado River bank. A fitting place for the new, six-year-old Territorial Prison. If a man was sent here he would certainly experience a foretaste of hell. Jay had visited Yuma in his travels when he had first come into the Territory. It had been at the tail end of a typical summer of withering, scorching heat, and he had not lingered. It was worse than anything he had ever experienced. He wondered why anyone would choose to live in such a climate. He guessed it must be for the pleasant, frost-free winter months — or the gold that had been discovered a few years previously upstream. A settlement had gradually grown up here because of the ferry — the only feasible crossing for miles in either direction before the building of the bridges. It was also at the point where the Gila River emptied into the Colorado.

How did this chase into the desert compare with hiring a fancy rig for the day from J. Tompkinson's Livery Stable on Minna Street in San Francisco? He and Fred had taken their girls for Saturday afternoon drives and picnics in Golden Gate Park. Maybe this wasn't exactly more fun, but it was certainly more adventurous. Chasing Yen Ching seemed to Jay like trying to catch a rattlesnake whose fangs one had just barely escaped. Why not let well enough alone? He was no policeman. Yet he had accepted this job and was presumably going to be paid for it. He got a sour taste in his mouth when he remembered the real reason he had been put on the payroll. A "decoy," Bassett had called him. He felt like a fool for being so gullible. He'd have a few choice words to say to Fred's police captain when, or if, he got back to San Francisco. This chase was liable to settle into a long drawn-out affair because of the answer that had come to their telegram last evening at 6:15 P.M. from the sheriff at Yuma. The reply was fairly brief. It stated that the station master had seen several Chinese getting off the train but had been busy and paid no attention to where they had gone. The two extra baggage cars had been sidetracked, and the train had pulled out. Several hired men had been seen unloading the freight cars of their boxes and loading them aboard the *Mohave II*, an upbound river sternwheeler. It was presumed the Chinese had gone upriver with their freight.

They were hot on the trail now. As Jay came inside off the coach's end platform and retrieved his grip as the train slowed to a stop, he only wished he had had more sleep. It was doubtful that he'd get much rest for some time to come.

"What's the plan, gentlemen?" Jay asked as they set their bags down on the depot platform. "Do we rent some horses or catch the next boat upstream?"

"The first thing we need to do is look up the sheriff we sent the wire to and get the details of what he knows," Fred said.

The sheriff of Yuma County turned out to be a whip-thin man who was several shades darker than the adobe buildings that dominated the town. He looked as if the sun had sucked all the juices out of him. He reminded Jay of a lean brown grasshopper who spat tobacco juice constantly. The big American-model Smith & Wesson he wore on his hip looked almost too heavy for him.

"Yup, they headed upstream on the *Mohave II*, a big sternwheeler, 'bout two days ago," the sheriff, who introduced himself as Bob Stafford, told them as he lounged back in his desk chair and clasped his hands behind his head.

"Any idea where they were headed?"

Stafford shook his head and shot a stream of brown juice at a nearby cuspidor, hit it dead center, and wiped his mouth with the back of his hand.

"Not really. If that was mining machinery in those crates, there are plenty of mines up there northeast of Ehrenberg." Without turning, he waved at the enlarged wall map behind him. "What did you say these men were wanted for, anyway?"

"Robbery. We think they're involved in the robbery of the United States Mint in San Francisco."

Sheriff Stafford nodded his head solemnly.

"Is there a livery stable in town where we can rent some horses?" Jay asked.

Stafford nodded. "If you're goin' after them on horseback, you've got some mighty rugged country to cross."

He got up from his desk and went to the wall map. "If you stay on the east side of the river you've got desert, and lava beds, and some really rough mountains. And the passages between them are full of all kinds of boulders and thorny cactus of every kind you can name. I've ridden up that way a few times. No roads. A man on horseback can't make no time at all. And I swear, it's rattlesnake heaven." He chuckled. "I admit, it looks simple on the map — just like you could cut across and save distance where the river makes this big loop to the west before she comes back.

But I know for a fact you'd make better time by riverboat. You can rent horses at Ehrenberg if you go that far."

"When's the next boat?" Bassett asked.

"There's one loading at the landing now," Stafford replied. "Probably be pullin' out in an hour or so. You got plenty o' time to get your tickets at the Colorado Steam Navigation Company office. You may have seen it when you come off the train. It's in the railroad depot at the foot of Main Street."

"They've got a two-day head start on us. I wonder if they're already at Ehrenberg? That's the most logical stop for them."

The sheriff looked at Bassett. "That's about a ninety-mile trip from here by river," he said. "And that river don't run straight. There's so many sandbars they don't run at night. At the best it'd take probably four days."

"Maybe we'd be better off going overland by horseback."

The sheriff shrugged. "It's up to you. But like I said, you've got the Chocolate Mountains and the Trigo Mountains between here and there, if you go the straightest course. If you swing east, away from the river, you've got the Castle Dome Mountains that are just as rugged. In either case you'd be lucky to make Ehrenberg in about the same length of time. So even if your horse doesn't break a leg in the rocks or you don't run out of water, you're still figurin' on roughly the same time as the boat. If it were me, I'd take the easy way and go by boat."

Jay was getting tired just listening to this dried-up lawman describe the rigors of travel in the desert mountains. "Let's go by boat," he suggested. The others agreed.

They thanked the sheriff, went out of the adobe office into the hot sun, and started for the ticket office at the depot.

They bought their tickets and carried their scant luggage aboard the *Gila*, the shallow-draft sternwheeler tied to the riverbank. There was no wharf. The roustabouts were just finishing offloading some barrels and boxes and sacks of assorted freight that had come up from a steamer on the Gulf of California below Port Ysabel. A group of Mexican and Indian laborers were stacking the goods into the beds of wagons when the trio went up the gangway. Jay could feel the zinc-covered deck burning his feet through his thin-soled boots as they showed their tickets to the mate. He directed them forward and up to the next deck to one of only four staterooms. The main deck was open for cargo, firewood for the steam engine, and the engine itself. The hurricane deck above the staterooms held only the pilothouse forward and a saloon behind, separated by a black smokestack towering overhead. Black smoke was boiling out of it and rising straight up as the boiler was kept hot and oil was added to the firebox in preparation for getting under way.

They threw their belongings on three of the four bunks in the small room and came back outside, looking for a breath of cool air. But there was none to be had. In the sultry air the Stars and Stripes hung limply from a flagstaff at the stern, and a blue, triangular pennant hung just as limply from a jackstaff at the bow.

Just as Jay had leaned on the rail, looking down at the roustabouts taking in the gangway, the blast of a steam whistle above startled him. The bowline was cast off a mooring post by a man on shore and hauled in by a deckhand.

The large paddlewheel began to splash slowly, backing the boat out into the river. Then the engine was reversed and the boat began its drive upriver, churning the chocolate-colored water behind it to foam.

The forward motion of the boat created at least a little breeze, and the trio stayed out on deck watching the scenery slide by.

"There's the Territorial Prison," Jay said, pointing at the squat stone-and-adobe complex that sprawled across the top of a flat, rocky bluff. The buff-colored buildings nearly blended into the rock of the bluff and the desert terrain surrounding it.

"Damn! I don't know how a *lizard* survives in that place in the summer," Fred Casey commented as they watched the dreaded prison move slowly past them.

"If it's this hot in late April, imagine what it must be in the summer," Bassett added.

"I was through here in August a couple of years back," Jay said. "Thought I was going to die. Next to the thought of hanging, I believe that prison would deter anybody who had a leaning toward a life of crime."

When Yuma had faded into the distance, they walked around the deck that circled the boat and gave their new quarters a good going-over. They discovered that they shared the boiler deck with only four other passengers: two young Army lieutenants and their wives, who were going up to Fort Mojave, where they were to travel overland to their new post at Fort Whipple. The *Gila* was less than one hundred feet long — considerably smaller than the *Mohave II*, they were told. A boat the size of the *Gila* could never have carried all of Yen Ching's crates. Jay had to assume that Yen Ching knew they were after him, but there was no telegraph between Yuma and Ehrenberg to warn anyone of their coming, so it was simply a chase. Jay couldn't imagine, when he thought about it or consulted the map Sheriff Stafford had given them of the river, how Yen Ching, two bodyguards, and a girl, presumably Lee Sing, would ever get very far with such a load of gold without getting cornered and caught. As he lay on his bunk trying to rest, it made no sense to him why they were going upstream into the interior instead of making a dash downstream toward the Gulf of California and a safe haven some-where in Mexico, as Yen Ching had told him. Maybe they didn't know exactly how to get there, since Yen Ching had wanted Jay to guide them. But Jay had been captured to guide them only to the Arizona-Mexico border.

Jay managed to doze off for a time, but he awoke bathed in perspiration. He got up and went out on deck, where Bassett and Casey were in conversation with the two lieutenants on the shady side of the boat. The talk was of various breeds of horses and their uses, and Jay drifted off to stroll alone around the boat again. The scenery on both sides of the river was monotonous. The reddish-brown water was bordered on both sides by a low line of cottonwoods and willows, and on the California side the low banks gave way to flat desert coun-try to the horizon, on the Arizona side to some jagged brown desert mountains in the distance.

The Army wives were not in evidence, apparently having retired to their cabins to rest, and the Mexican and Indian roustabouts were on the main deck try-ing to stay out of the way and comfort-able. There was nothing to enliven the dull afternoon. Jay wished he had brought something to read but had not thought of it in the rush to get to the boat. He considered climbing up to the pilothouse and engaging the captain in conversation but decided this might be a serious breach of etiquette. One did not enter the confines of a pilothouse on a riverboat without an invitation. He grew tired of staring at the whirlpools swirling in the treacherous red current and at the flat, green-bordered shore-line.

Suppertime finally came, announced by the ringing of a bell. The officers in their shirtsleeves, and their wives in the lightest cotton dresses, showed the three of them the way to the saloon, just aft of the pilothouse where the meals were served. The man serving as both cook and steward was Chinese. At the first sight of him Jay's stomach tensed. He wondered how long it would take to get him over this instinctive reaction to any male Oriental. This man was lean, with very slanted eyes. He obviously carried the weight of many years, but was still as spry as a much younger man.

The fare was not fancy, but filling and

reasonably good. Fresh biscuits with no butter, salt boiled beef, some canned tomatoes. This was followed by pies made from dried peaches.

"Damned good food, considering the conditions that Chinaman must be working under," Fred Casey said, helping himself to a second piece of pie.

The sun had gone down before they ate, and shortly after supper the light began to fail to the point that the pilot, whoever he was, began to ease in toward the right bank to tie up for the night. Jay could see that there was no running this river in the dark, what with its wicked current and its many snags, shoals, and sandbars.

This assessment was confirmed by the captain, Jack Mellon, after the *Gila* was firmly secured by hawsers to a small cottonwood on the bank and the crackling and fizzing of the high-pressure engines had died down for the night.

The late Spring heat had made the cabins intolerable, so all seven passengers had dragged the mattresses off their bunks and taken them up to place them, side by side, on the after part of the upper deck.

Captain Mellon, who had taken some

food in the pilothouse as he worked, now came down to talk to the passengers as they bedded down for the night.

"I've been running this river for more years than I care to remember. And it's something I hardly dare try, lights or no lights. The sandbars are constantly shifting. The river's falling just now, and if I put her hard on a bar we might lose a lot more time than we will by tying up each night. It's tough enough in daylight, but at night it's impossible."

"Even with a full moon, Captain?" one of the pretty young wives asked, glancing up at the handsome, dark-haired Mellon.

"Even with a full moon, ma'am."

"How many days to Ehrenberg?" Glen Bassett asked.

Captain Mellon shrugged. "Maybe five days, maybe less if we get lucky."

"After all your experience you can't gauge it any closer than that?" Bassett pressed. Jay thought he sounded a little irritable, probably from the heat, the flies, and lack of sleep.

"If there's one thing I learned since I ran away to sea at the age of ten, it's not to worry about things you have no control over," Jack Mellon replied evenly.

"We'll be casting off in the morning as soon as it's light enough to see. And since it's been a very long day I'll bid you all a good night. Ladies . . ." He gave the women in their thin sleeping gowns a gallant bow and turned away into the darkness toward his own quarters.

Jay stretched out on his mattress and clasped his hands behind his head, staring up at the stars overhead. From below on the main deck he could hear some low voices conversing in Spanish and an occasional laugh. A faint warm breeze brought the smell of the thick stands of arrowweed along the river bank.

This isn't San Francisco, but it's not half bad so far, he thought as he began to relax into a doze.

Finally he slept, a deep and contented sleep which would not have been possible had he known of what was ahead.

CHAPTER 15

It was three days later when Jay spotted her. The bell for supper had just been struck, and he was going forward toward the ladder that led to the upper deck. He happened to look over the starboard rail to a low, brush-covered island they were passing in the middle of the river. His eyes caught a movement in the thick mesquite. He stopped and looked closer. They had occasionally seen Cocopah or Yuma Indian women peering at the passing boat from the bushes along the shoreline, but this one must have canoed to the island for some reason.

When the *Gila* was nearly abreast of the low island, the figure moved out of the brush with her arms up. Her black hair hung in her face as she staggered forward a few steps and fell on the sandy strip of beach. From this distance she looked to be Indian, but she was wearing some very dirty and torn clothing that was definitely not the native dress of the area.

Jay dashed up the steps to the pilothouse, shouting for Captain Mellon to stop the boat.

"There's a woman on that island who's in trouble!"

Mellon asked no questions. He yanked the signal cord and opened the speaking tube and yelled down to the mate/engineer to stop the engine. A few seconds later the thrashing of the paddlewheel ceased and the boat's momentum slowed quickly as the current caught it. They drifted to a stop at the upper end of the long, narrow island.

"Slow forward!" Mellon ordered down the tube. He put the wheel over and the current caught the bow and slowly swung it in toward the island, as the boat drifted backward with only slight steerageway.

Through the open pilothouse windows Jay could see the roustabouts on the foredeck, looking up to see what the captain was up to. Then one or two of them spotted the woman crawling weakly along the edge of the water.

The bow swung in and ground softly

on the starboard side in the soft sand and mud.

Jay was out of the wheelhouse and bounding down the ladders to the main deck before the first deckhand leaped off.

One deckhand was heaving off the heavy mooring line to another hand on the bank when Jay leaped off the bow to sink up to his ankles in the soft red mud. He pulled loose, ran down the beach about thirty yards, and knelt beside the woman who was lying, facedown, on the sand. He gently rolled her over and brushed the hair and sand from her face. He caught his breath from shock. It was Lee Sing!

She was unconscious, her hair was hanging loose, and she was dressed in a torn, mud-streaked dress of Oriental design. But there was no mistaking that face.

Jay was amazed at how she seemed almost weightless as he scooped her up and carried her to the boat. Willing hands lifted her to the deck and then helped him back aboard, as the passengers, who had abandoned their meal, were leaning over the upper rail to see what was going on.

The girl was carried to one of two vacant cabins and brought around with a few sips of brandy administered by Captain Mellon. When her eyes fluttered open, she smiled and squeezed Jay's hand and nodded to Fred Casey. Everyone had crowded into the cabin to see what the muddy Colorado had given them. Lee Sing was put in charge of the two Army wives to get her cleaned up and into some dry clothes. She did not speak but seemed fairly alert, even though weak.

"Get the Chinese cook to see if he can talk to her," Mellon said to one of the deckhands.

"Never mind, Captain," Jay said. "This girl speaks perfect English."

"You know her?" The pilot arched his eyebrows at him.

"Yes. I'll tell you about it later."

"Get the cook anyway," Mellon ordered. "This girl needs some food."

The captain ran everyone out of the cabin except the two women.

A few minutes later the *Gila* was once again plowing northward up the river and the passengers were back at their meal in the saloon. Jay said nothing at the table, but could hardly wait until they were finished so he could get his two companions alone.

"At least we know for sure we're on the trail of Yen Ching," he told Fred and Glen when they had retreated to the boiler deck after supper.

"I could hardly believe my eyes," Fred Casey said, picking his teeth as he leaned against a stanchion. "What do you suppose happened to her?"

"Did they try to kill her?" Bassett asked.

"Could be," Jay nodded. "Maybe Yen Ching tired of her, or she did something to infuriate him. He has an unpredictable and violent temper."

"Or she might have escaped from him, like she did before," Fred speculated.

"How long could she have been on that island?" Jay asked.

"We'll have to wait until she gets some food and rest before we question her," Bassett said.

"She didn't appear to be seriously injured. I noticed just a few cuts and scratches."

That evening, when the boat had nosed into the bank and tied up for the night, Jay and Fred gave the whole story to Captain Mellon in his cabin.

"So you can see that this girl is a vital witness against the Chee Kong tong and the robbery at the Mint. But we still have to have evidence; we have to find the gold they took."

"Amazing story," Mellon mused when they finished. "I've seen and heard a lot of wild things on this river in my time, but this about tops them all." He scratched a match across his heel to light his pipe.

They had checked on Lee Sing earlier and found that she had been given some hot beef broth and small pieces of bread. When Jay and Fred had looked in on her she was lying on the bunk in an exhausted sleep, with one of the women watching over her.

"She'll probably sleep through the night," the woman told them.

And that proved to be the case. She awoke in the morning, ravenous. But her stomach had shrunk and she could eat only a small amount of what the Chinese cook brought before she felt stuffed. She smiled and said something to him in Chinese when he came to take away her dishes. He gave her a quick reply in their native tongue, and a smile creased his ancient face as he went out the cabin door.

Fred had asked the Army wife who had spent the night with Lee Sing to leave for a few minutes so they could talk to her in private. The woman seemed a little miffed at this even when Fred showed her his police badge, but she departed, leaving the three men to talk to Lee Sing.

"Jay McGraw," she said, using his full name as she always did, "it is good to see you again." The voice still had that musical quality he had first noted, yet now it sounded weaker. Impulsively, he went over and gave her a quick hug as she sat up on the bed.

"Why are you here?" she asked when he drew away.

"We were after you and Yen Ching."

"How did you know . . . ?" she began, but Jay raised his hand.

"No, tell me first what happened to you."

"They took me from the mission."

"I know. We heard how they tricked Mrs. Frierson."

"I was taken to a secret place where Yen Ching and other members of the Chee Kong tong were hiding. Later, I was taken to the docks and put on a ship. I thought we were going back to China, but —"

"What happened to the gold?" Bassett interrupted.

"I heard later it was hidden in the coffins of the dead bodies of our people."

"Just as we guessed!" Fred exploded. "Where is it now?"

"The bodies were removed from the boxes on the ship and some kinds of tools were put in them. I never saw the gold because I was not allowed anywhere near the hold. Yen Ching kept me close to him at all times. When he had to leave to attend to something, he left one of the boo how doy to guard me. He did not trust me after my escape. I know these things only because I heard Yen Ching talking to his guards when he thought I was asleep. We were on the ship maybe three days when the engines stopped and I was able to see we were in port. I knew we had not been at sea long enough to reach China. A few days later I was taken ashore at night and put on a train. Then we got off at the town on the river, and I saw that many of these boxes were unloaded from the train and loaded onto a boat. The boxes were marked with English labels that said they contained mining machinery. I did not see the gold, but it must be in those crates."

"Why are they going *up* the river instead of into Mexico?" Jay asked.

"I do not know. They told me nothing. All I could find out was by listening when they did not know it."

"How did you get away from them? What were you doing on that island?"

She shook her head and rubbed a hand over her eyes before she replied, and Jay noted how much thinner she looked than he remembered.

"I did not know where we were going, but I waited and watched and listened for a chance to get away. Yen Ching kept me locked in the cabin with him. They brought my food and water to me. It was very hot in the cabin, and I begged to be let out on the deck because there was no place I could go. But he would not. I was frightened. Yen Ching was becoming more and more cruel to me. I decided I would rather be killed by his guards or die in the desert than live like I was being forced to live. I watched for a chance. Finally, on the third day, Yen Ching was asleep in the bunk and one of his guards started to come into the cabin. I was pretending to sleep on the other bunk. As he opened the door he turned to say something to the other boo how doy, and I ran past him and jumped over the railing into the river."

"By God," Bassett breathed.

"I went down deep under that warm, muddy water and tried not to breathe for a long time. I came up and took a breath and they saw me. The big wheel had stopped turning. They were pointing at me, but I saw where I was and swam down under the water again and tried to go toward the shore, but the current was pushing me along and I was bumping on the bottom. I finally had to come up to breathe again and I was on the other side of the boat and a way off from it. They were all on the other side of the boat, and I was able to swim to this island and hide in the reeds along the shore. I could not swim well because of the dress I was wearing. But they finally gave up looking for me and the boat went on."

"Captain Mellon told us that there is a saying on this river that whatever disappears beneath its muddy red waters is never seen again," Jay said. "You've just disproved *that.*"

"I was very tired and very frightened," she continued. "I crawled up onto the island and stayed there. There was nothing to eat there but a few lizards, and I was not able to catch them. There was shade in the bushes, and I drank water from the river."

"How long were you there?"

"About four days. No other boats passed. I got so very hungry at first. Later, I was very tired and slept a lot. I was sleeping when I heard your boat coming. I was just able to get out to the bank, and then I don't remember what happened."

"Yen Ching bought tickets for Ehrenberg. Do you know if that is where they really plan to stop?"

She shook her head. "I do not know. I'm sorry."

Jay squeezed her hand. "That's okay. Get some rest. We'll talk more later."

She gave him a wan smile and laid her head back on the pillow.

CHAPTER 16

It was days before the Gila reached Ehrenberg — days of increasing heat and the almost constant aggravation of groundings on sandbars. In spite of Jack Mellon's best efforts and experience the reddish current of the tricky Colorado hid the newly formed mud- and sandbars until the bow had grounded. In suspected shallow water the Mexican deckhands stood on the bow with long poles and tested the depth, drawling out the water depths. Often one of them would suddenly cry out, *"No alli agua!"* Then they would leap over the side into waist-deep water and help push the bow as the captain reversed the big paddlewheel. But in spite of their constant vigilance the boat was delayed more than thirty hours by groundings.

Finally, at mid-morning on a hot, cloudless day, the town of Ehrenberg came into sight on the Arizona side. Jay was glad of the delays for one reason: they had given Lee Sing time to recover her strength and gain a little weight. The elderly Chinese cook doted on her and could not have been more helpful or attentive, bringing her special dishes he prepared. So by the time the boat nosed in toward dreary-looking Ehrenberg she stood at the rail with the men to see where she was about to land. They had discussed whether or not she should stay out of sight at first, until it was learned if Yen Ching and his men were there. But the boat was landing only briefly, and there was literally no place to hide from anyone who might be watching the landing. Jay could hardly credit Captain Mellon's statement that this drab settlement of only a few adobe houses was a major freighting point for parties continuing inland.

They gathered their few belongings, checked their guns, and shook hands with the Army couples and with Jack Mellon, who had come down from the pilothouse to have a smoke and stretch his legs as the passengers departed.

"Hope you catch this Chinaman you're after," Mellon said. "I'd hate to think some foreigner got away with three million dollars from the United States Treasury. I sure wish I could see how this comes out." He glanced up the slope toward the settlement. "I know I don't have to tell you to be very careful. You know your job. But take care of that girl, Lee Sing. We snatched her alive from the river, but I wouldn't press my luck."

"Don't worry, Captain," Jay said. "If they get her, they'll have to get me first." As soon as he'd said it, Jay felt foolish at this show of bravado.

As they walked off the gangway and up the river bank, two of the men abreast and Bassett behind with Lee Sing, Jay half expected to hear a rifle crack from the town above. Except for a few Mexicans unloading supplies from the boat, there was no one to be seen. But Jay could not shake the prickly feeling that was going up the back of his neck. Someone had to be watching them from behind the adobe walls ahead. His left hand held his small grip and his right he kept near the pearl butt of his holstered Colt.

But they made the town without incident. The one main street of the settlement ran along parallel to the river at the top of the river bank, and a few cross streets went off at right angles to it between the buildings before straggling off into the desert after a block or two.

They paused on the main street, unsure of which way to go.

"There's no official representative of the law here," Jay said. "Only one soldier stationed at a place called the Government House."

"Let's take a look at this place first," Jay suggested. "If we don't see anything of the Chinaman, we can check the freight house. That must be that big building over there."

It was only a matter of about fifteen minutes to walk through the whole town. Their first impression had been accurate: dusty and drab, with nearly all the buildings made of adobe. Several Mexican and Indian children were playing in the streets, accompanied by a few dogs. The handful of adults they saw were either walking or astride small donkeys. The tops of two trees appeared over the white wall surrounding the Government House patio, but other than that not a tree or blade of grass was in sight. There was a Mexican bakery, a barber shop, a saloon, a large livery with both animals and wagons for hire, and James Barney's store. It was an adobe structure, with a wooden awning supported by several posts shading the front of the place and the few loafers who lounged beneath it.

They drew some curious glances, but no one spoke to them. They walked back to the big freight house they had passed, where they found a blond white man in the office, hunched over a stack of papers on his desk.

"What can I do for you?" he asked, looking up as their bodies blocked the daylight in the open doorway. Jay and Lee Sing were the last in and Jay maneuvered her inside.

"We're looking for some Chinese men who may have stored some crates of mining machinery in your warehouse in the past few days," Fred Casey said.

"And who might you be?" the man asked, glancing at the four of them, his eyes nesting on Lee Sing.

Casey introduced the three of them as law officers and showed his identification. "One of the men was very fat."

"Yes, some men like that got off the boat a few days ago," the blond man said, leaning back in his chair. "But they didn't do any business with me. You might check over at the livery. I believe they hired two or three wagons and hauled their stuff east."

They thanked him and trudged back to the livery stable they had passed earlier. It consisted of a five-foot adobe wall enclosing a square of about one hundred and fifty feet on a side. About half the enclosure was roofed with willows and brush supported by posts set in the hard earth. But the roof was free-standing, and about nine feet high to admit any breeze that might be blowing.

"Yes, *señor,* such men as you describe rented two ore wagons from me a few days past," the stocky Mexican owner told them when Fred had shown him his police badge. "They paid me in gold."

"In gold?"

"Yes, *señor.*"

"I'd like to see some of those coins."

The Mexican shrugged. "I'm sorry, *señor,* but I no longer have them. I paid for a large shipment of grain and hay with it. The money is gone downriver."

"You say they loaded some crates on these wagons?"

"*Si.* They hired several of my men and

those who stay around Barney's store to help them."

"Did they pay these men in gold, too?"

"No, *señor*. They were paid in greenbacks. I remember because one of my workers wanted to purchase one of my twenty-dollar gold pieces from me to give to his wife."

"Did you sell it?"

"No, *señor*."

"It wouldn't make any difference anyway, Fred," Jay said. "I've already seen some 1882 double eagles in circulation, so it's not like these are going to be unique."

"Which way did they go when they left here?" Bassett asked.

"North."

"North? Along the river? They didn't go east?"

The Mexican shook his head firmly. "When they pulled out of here with my mules hauling the wagons, they went straight north along the top of the riverbank."

They questioned him for a few more minutes, but he could add nothing to what he had already told them.

In deference to Lee Sing, who was not up to riding astride, they rented a light spring wagon and a span of mules from the Mexican. They threw their scant luggage into it and, with Jay handling the reins and the long whip, pulled out of the enclosure and swung into the main street.

Since they didn't know exactly where they were going or how long they would be gone, Jay pulled up in front of Barney's store and they bought a few supplies: frying pan, matches, bacon, a sack of beans, some cornmeal, three large, blanket-covered canteens, four blankets, and two boxes of cartridges to fit their revolvers.

They parked their rig at the side of the store to be out of the way of two prospectors out front who were loading a wagon with what looked to be six months' worth of supplies. Jay, at his own insistence, had done all the shopping while the rest of them browsed through the store. With Jay's offhand manner and innocent questions, asked as if he were just passing the time of day, he was able to wheedle all kinds of information from the store clerk. He had a knack for this which he had found very useful in the past. When they returned to the wagon with the box of supplies, he had obtained more than groceries and camp gear.

He took the reins once more and guided the mules north out of town, past a graveyard with its wooden headboards, as rocky and desolate as the burial ground next to the Territorial Prison.

"Get out that map of the river the sheriff gave us," Jay said over his shoulder. "It's in my bag there."

"Where you headed?" Bassett asked, reaching over the back of the seat for the leather grip.

"Found out there's a ghost town about seven miles north of here — Laguna de la Paz. Peaceful Lake. It sprang up about the time the Civil War started when they discovered a lot of placer gold and nuggets. The place was on a backwater of the Colorado and that's how it got its name. Everybody later shortened the name to La Paz. But the clerk said it was anything but peaceful. One of the wildest boom towns in the Territory. In fact, it was the county seat until the gold gave out and the county seat was moved down to Yuma in 1868. It may be on the map."

"Yiiaahhh!!" Bassett leapt backward,

nearly falling over the front seat.

"What's wrong?" Startled, Jay yanked the mules to a halt.

"A rattlesnake in your bag!" Bassett shouted, staggering upright again with the help of Casey. "Damn near got me!"

A faint buzzing sound came from the back of the wagon. Jay leapt off the seat and ran around to the back. His small leather grip still rested upright, the top only slightly open. A buzzing rattle came from inside.

"Did he get you?" Jay asked, noting the sickly pale look on Bassett's face.

"No. I've got to sit down." He sank down weakly on the backseat. "When I opened the bag, I guess he couldn't throw himself into a coil quick enough to strike before I saw him and jumped back." He pointed to the back of the rear seat. "That's where he struck," he said weakly.

Two glistening drops of venom were slowly trickling down the back of the wooden seat.

Jay took the butt of the buggy whip, slid the bag over to the tailgate, and dropped it off onto the ground, where it fell on its side. He carefully lifted one flap of the top with the whip, and they watched as a small desert rattlesnake slithered out, coiled, and cocked its head, its upright tail buzzing fiercely. Jay reversed the whip and lashed at it a time or two. The snake dropped and slithered away, making figure S's in the sand as it crawled quickly away and disappeared under a bush at the side of the road.

"Not very big to be so damn mean," Fred Casey said.

"Sidewinder," Jay said. "They don't get very big."

"How did it get into your bag?" Bassett asked.

"Was it buckled shut?" Jay asked.

"Sure was. In fact, one of the buckles was stuck and I had a little trouble getting it open. He didn't crawl in there by accident. Somebody put him there."

"Probably somebody's idea of a joke. Maybe one of those loafers in front of Barney's store."

"Let's go back and find out," Casey said, his face reddening. "They probably thought we wouldn't find it until we camped tonight."

"I'm for it, for whatever good it'll do," Bassett said, still shaky. "We're only about a half-mile out of town."

Jay poured out the contents of his bag and the other bags first, to be sure they were free of any further surprises such as scorpions, then repacked them and pulled the team around.

They identified themselves as law officers to the loafers in front of Barney's before they waded in with questions. But the Mexicans, who spoke only little English, protested their innocence with such conviction that Jay was almost inclined to believe them. Two white men were there also, one of whom was old and sported a white beard.

"Did you see anyone near our wagon when we were in the store?" Jay demanded of the white men.

"Warn't rightly payin' much attention, mister," the old man said. "Lots of strangers pass by here, especially when the boats is dockin' and leavin'."

"This was less than an hour ago. *Think*, man!"

The old man stroked his beard with one hand and pondered the question. "Yore wagon was around t' the side, warn't it? I don't recollect seein' nobody around that way." He paused. "Did see a Chinaman on a horse pass by, though."

"A Chinaman?" Jay could hardly conceal his excitement.

"Yeah," the man replied slowly. "He went on around thataway past yore wagon and I didn't see him come back. I recollect 'cause he was a funny sight, all dressed in some kind of black, quilted-lookin' outfit with a black hat. Don't see many Chinamen around here."

Jay thanked him, and the four of them climbed back into the wagon. Jay slapped the reins over the mules.

"That explains it," Fred said when they were out of earshot. "One of the boo how doy."

"Yes, it must be," Lee Sing said. "They know you are following. It was a warning."

"Maybe thought they'd kill one of us, or force us to turn around and look for a doctor in a hurry. Maybe delay us for a time."

They fell silent for a few minutes as the ominous threat of the deadly serpent worked on their imaginations. What would be next, Jay wondered? There was certainly no element of surprise left on the pursuers' side. They would have to watch every step they made from here on.

"Well, let's have a look at that map," Jay said finally to break the gloomy silence.

"Yeh, here's La Paz," Casey said, smoothing the map over his knee to hold it steady on the bouncing rig.

"So there's a ghost town just north of here. What of it?" Bassett asked.

Jay shrugged. "Just a hunch. The deliveryman said they headed north out of town. And" — he grinned over his shoulder — "I've been following the deep ruts of what appear to be some heavily loaded wagons for the past five minutes."

The two men and Lee Sing immediately began looking down and ahead. Where the soil was soft and sandy, the wheel marks of wagons and many hooves were plain to see. The ground turned rocky and the tracks disappeared for a few minutes, only to pick up again a couple of hundred yards farther on where the desert wind had blown the sandy soil across what had evidently been a road in years past.

"Nothing could be plainer than that. A blind man could follow it."

"Yeah. It's a little too plain to suit me," Fred Casey said, loosening the .38 in its holster and looking around nervously. But there was nothing to see except the river and its bordering trees on their left, desert to their right dotted with mesquite and palo verde, and the blue-gray outlines of distant desert mountains ahead of them.

About an hour later the adobe ruins of La Paz came into view. As forlorn and desolate as Ehrenberg had looked, this place was ten times worse. Mesquite bushes sprouted in the one main street. Roofless adobe buildings were gradually melting back into the desert, since most roofs and doors had been scavenged for their scarce wood by other builders. Vacant windows and doorways gaped at them as they silently drove down the main street. The backwater lagoon that had given the town its name could be seen a hundred yards to the left, downslope between two buildings. It had long since been silted in by the raging floodwaters of the muddy Colorado — the main reason for the town's demise, along with the diminishing of placer gold.

Jay's eyes shifted to the ground again. Marks of the only recent visitors were plain to see, since wind and rain had scoured away all other tracks from the once busy street. He drove the mules slowly to the end of the street, where the tracks of the heavy wagons made a big loop and started back into town. Jay did likewise. After traversing the street twice he pulled the team to a halt, set the brake, looped the reins around the brake handle and climbed down. "I want to look around a little."

Not that there was much to see. Iron doors and shutters from what had once been banks and mercantile establishments lay half-buried in heaps of crumbled rock and brick and scaling rust. In front of one of the larger buildings a wooden sign still hung by one end. The board was warped and the paint was peeling but Jay could make out part of the name: GOLDWATER & . . . The remainder of the writing had been obliterated by weathering.

The other three got out of the wagon and followed as Jay walked to the end of the street, looking at the ruined buildings and the tracks of the ore wagons and shod mules.

"I can't figure out what they were doing," he said finally, coming to a stop with his hand on the butt of his gun.

The sound of his own voice was strange in the deathly silence. Not even a breeze was stirring to rustle the mesquite bushes that were taking over the place. "It looks like they just drove up and down the street."

They made another careful search of both sides of the street from end to end.

"Here are some footprints," Bassett said. "Looks like they got down here and did a lot of walking around, in and out of some of these buildings."

"And it looks like they brushed out most of their tracks inside here," Fred Casey added as he came out of an empty building. "See . . . here." He pointed to where a branch, broken off a mesquite bush, was lying on the ground, its leaves beginning to wither in the hot sun.

They all walked inside one of the roofless adobes. Nothing seemed disturbed or changed. If the place had had a wooden floor it was long since gone. The sandy earth was all that remained.

"That gold could be hidden somewhere around here," Fred said. "Why else would they be fooling around in a ghost town?"

"They've done a lot of things so far to throw us off the trail."

"Let's see if we can pick up those wagon tracks," Jay said, walking out into the street again. "They can't hide those for very long."

"Uh-oh!" Fred Casey was staring off to the northeast.

"What's wrong?"

"Look there." He pointed toward the horizon.

"What is it?" Bassett asked, squinting in the sunlight. "Looks like a funny cloud."

"It's a dust storm," Jay said. "And it's coming fast."

A low brown cloud that stretched across most of the northeast horizon was boiling toward them, rising higher in the sky with each passing second.

"We'd better get the team to some shelter so they don't panic."

Jay and Fred led the mules and wagon between two closely spaced buildings and secured their reins to a rusty iron pipe protruding from a pile of debris. This done, they soaked their bandannas from the canteens and tied them over their own faces, covering their mouths and noses.

"Let's get in there. This will block the worst of it," Jay said, leading the three into a ruined adobe building. By now the sun was only a dull disk in the afternoon sky, and an eerie twilight had settled over the place.

A faint puff of wind stirred the still air, then another, a little stronger. From inside the roofless walls Jay looked out an empty window and saw the wind kicking up loose sand and bending the mesquite bushes in gusts as the full fury of the storm hit them. It grew darker as they huddled against the wall, faces averted from the stinging blast of wind-driven sand and eyes shut against the clouds of dust that swirled down and around them. There was little Jay could do to protect Lee Sing. They would all have to ride it out. He put his arms around her and tucked her head in the hollow of his shoulder so she could breathe a little easier in the lee of the blast of fine grit. He could smell and taste the dirt through the damp bandanna.

Jay and Lee Sing were standing about five feet inside the doorway that opened out to the back of the building.

Suddenly he was hit in the backs of

the legs and he and the girl went down. At the same instant something whistled over his head and hit the wall. He twisted as he fell to keep from landing on the girl. Fred had knocked them clear or a cleaver would have beheaded him. The hatchet man, dressed in black, was yanking his weapon out of the crumbling adobe wall for another throw. Fred grabbed his revolver.

"Damn!" The sand had jammed the mechanism. He rolled out of the way as the highbinder swung the heavy blade at him. Fred snatched the Colt Lightning from Jay's holster and squeezed the trigger. The weapon exploded in the face of the hatchet man and he fell forward over Fred. The cleaver flew from his hand striking Glen Bassett in the leg and then it fell to the ground. Bassett screamed out in pain.

"Are there any more of them?" Casey yelled over the roar of the wind, shoving clear of the dead Chinaman and springing to his feet.

"Let's get out of here." They took hold of Lee Sing and Bassett. "We can't leave until this storm blows over, but let's get outside. At least nobody can slip up on us there."

Fred Bassett was lying on the ground, gripping his left leg where the razor-sharp cleaver had split his pants leg and sliced a long cut on the side of his lower leg. It was bleeding profusely.

They helped him out into the street where they crouched back to back, guns drawn, red eyes slitted against the dust and sand. They washed Bassett's leg wound with canteen water and bound it with his one clean spare shirt from his small handbag. The bleeding subsided and the pain was tolerable. Finally, it was all settled.

"This is one of Yen Ching's bodyguards," Lee Sing said with no emotion when they went back inside the building and rolled over the dead man. "His name is Harm Ah Kee. Ah Kow is the other guard who is traveling with him. They are both very bad men."

"This one isn't anymore," Casey remarked grimly.

"What's our next move?" Bassett asked.

"Follow those freight wagons. Yen Ching and his henchman can't be very far from here. They must have left this one behind to take care of us."

They walked outside again. But all

footprints had been smoothed away as if they had never existed, and there was no trace of the tracks left by the freight wagons.

CHAPTER 17

"Well, so much for that idea," Jay said with some disgust. "First things first, though. We need to get our mules to water."

"I thought I saw a faint trace of smoke coming up from those trees along the river about a half-mile upstream," Fred said. "I couldn't be sure, it was gone so quickly."

"If we go down to the river we may be walking into a trap," Bassett said.

"Or it could be some of the river Indians. Maybe the Yumas. They've been friendly for years."

They retrieved their team of mules and wiped the mud out of their nostrils with wet bandannas, then shared some of their water from the canteens with the animals, letting them drink from Jay's hat.

Then Jay led the mules, still hitched to the wagon, out of town, down the slope toward the river to where some sparse grass was growing, uphill from the thick stands of willow and cotton-wood that lined the river bank. He slipped the bits out of their mouths and, taking care to keep the wagon between himself and the river, let them graze for a half hour or more. He was taking no chances on the team's being stolen or of his being shot from ambush.

Then he led them back to the flat, open desert area just out of the vacant town, where he and Fred unhitched the team, hobbled their front feet, and let them roll in the sand and hop around, nibbling at the mesquite.

An hour before sundown they built a fire and cooked up some supper of corn cakes and bacon, washed down with water from their canteens. The meal over, the utensils were scoured with sand and the fire smothered.

"It won't do for us to be sitting around a bright campfire after dark," Casey remarked, kicking sand on the smoking embers. "Lee can sleep in the wagon and the rest of us on the ground while one stands guard. We'll rotate it about two hours each."

"I'll take most of the watch," Bassett

offered. "This leg won't let me get much sleep anyway. Besides, I'm not used to sleeping on the ground."

"Maybe we ought to go back and bury that dead highbinder," Fred said, eyeing the three or four black silhouettes soaring about three hundred feet overhead.

"Hell, let the buzzards have him," Bassett gritted, gingerly feeling his wrapped leg.

"I think we should bury him," Jay agreed. "What can we use for a shovel?"

Casey shrugged. "We'll find something in all that junk scattered around."

They left Bassett and Lee Sing by the wagon and walked back into the empty town. In a pile of trash behind one of the buildings they found two four-foot-long iron rods and a frying pan with a hole in it. There was also a large piece of a broken crockery bowl.

The remains of Harm Ah Kee were lying faceup where he had been left. They found his hat and placed it over his face.

"No sense carrying him anyplace," Jay remarked.

"Let's plant him where he fell," Fred agreed. "Provided the ground isn't too hard in here."

They searched the body first and pulled a .45 Colt single-action from the waistband, under the black jumper.

"Wonder why he didn't use that on us instead of the cleaver?" Jay said, checking the load and then setting the gun aside.

"Hard to say, unless the blade was quieter and he didn't want to take a chance on it misfiring, like mine did," Casey replied. "Or maybe splitting your skull was more traditional."

"I'm just glad you saw him in time," Jay said, getting down on his knees and beginning to chop at the sandy soil with the piece of jagged crockery.

"This ground's pretty soft," Casey remarked, jabbing at it with one of the iron rods.

"Mostly sand," Jay said.

"We won't get it real deep if it keeps collapsing."

"We can knock a few of these adobes down on top of it afterwards to keep the varmits off."

They worked for a few minutes in silence.

"Oh no!"

"What?"

"I think I hit a rock. Some luck. Wonder if there's a ledge under here, or if we can just move over a few feet and be clear of it."

Jay scooped out the dirt and sand with the frying pan. Then he brushed the sand away with his hands. "It's not a rock. It's just some old iron pipe. Reckon they piped water up here from the river somehow?"

He dug along the section of pipe a foot in each direction. "No, here's the end of it. It's only a single piece."

"Well, yank it up outa there and let's get on with it."

"Ugh! Gimme a hand. This thing must be made of lead instead of hollow iron."

"Probably full of sand."

But the two-foot section of pipe was plugged at both ends with some kind of tarry substance. They threw the pipe aside and continued digging. Less than a foot to one side they struck another identical piece.

"What is this stuff, anyway?" Fred wondered aloud. "It sure doesn't look like it's been in the ground very long."

"You can't tell by the way it looks," Jay said. "Metal can last indefinitely in this desert. The only reason some of that stuff in the junk pile out back is rusted is because of the dampness near this river. Something like this pipe buried in the ground might never rust."

By the time they had pulled the third section of pipe from under the earthen floor their curiosity was aroused.

"These things must be filled with lead, as heavy as they are," Casey remarked, pulling one end of a pipe toward him and opening his jacknife. Jay paused in his digging, wiping the sweat from his brow to watch.

"This is the kind of stuff they use to caulk wooden ships," he remarked, digging at the tarry substance.

When he finally got the end of the pipe clear, he tilted the other end. Nothing came out.

"There's gotta be something in there; it's too heavy to be hollow. Give me a rock or something to break this. I'm not sticking my hand in there where I can't see."

They lugged the pipe outside, where they found a rectangular piece of granite someone had used for a doorstep.

"Okay. On the count of three. One, two, three!"

They flung the heavy pipe across the straight edge of the granite rock. The cast iron cracked open and two cloth sacks fell out. They both moved forward, slowly, as if afraid to touch them.

Fred lifted one of the sacks. "This is it, Jay! This it *it!*" U.S. TREASURY was stenciled in black across the white canvas bag.

They looked at each other unbelievingly. Then Jay grabbed up the other sack and untied the drawstring. He up-ended the bag, and a cascade of gold coins came pouring out onto the polished granite with a ringing clash of metal. Coins bounced and rolled off in all directions.

They both knelt and scooped up handfuls of the identical double eagles.

"By damn! Isn't that a sight!"

"Takes my breath away."

The setting sun caught the dull gleam of the gold on the rock. The image seemed frozen in time. They stared at it, stunned for a few seconds.

Finally, Jay shook himself loose and picked up one of the coins. The head of Liberty was finely struck on the obverse side, with the date, 1882, at the bottom. On the reverse, below the spread eagle, was a small *s* — the San Francisco Mint mark. He began picking up the coins and returning them to the sack. "We were right on top of it and never knew it."

"Maybe that hatchet man was making sure we didn't."

"I don't think so. I believe he was trying to kill me as a disloyal tong member and Lee Sing as a disloyal mistress."

"Well, whatever the reason, if he hadn't attacked we wouldn't be burying somebody and wouldn't have found it."

"How did just two of them and the fat man bury all that gold?" Jay asked as they carried the bags back inside the roofless adobe.

"They had a three-day head start on us, and they probably had shovels in those crates as well."

"You're right. Two men could do it in that time, since it was all sealed in those short pipes, and they weren't buried more than a foot deep."

"Old La Paz was never so rich, even in its boom days," Fred remarked.

"Let's take these two bags with us back to camp and re-bury the rest," Jay suggested.

"Good. What about this guy?" He jerked his head at the dead highbinder.

"Outside in the street. The sand has drifted there. We can use the mules to pull down the adobe wall over him in the morning." He looked at the sack in his hand. "Why don't we just retrieve a few of these sacks and ride off somewhere without telling anybody anything?" A wistful, faraway look came over his face.

"Yeah," Fred grinned. "But don't even think too much about it or it could really start working on you. Gold fever is a real disease. I've seen it ruin healthy men, even when they were after gold that didn't already belong to somebody."

As the long twilight was deepening into dusk they trudged back into camp, each swinging a small but heavy canvas sack and sporting a grin that could be seen from several yards away.

Glen Bassett was sitting on a blanket, his back against a wheel of the wagon, his Colt in his lap.

When Fred and Jay blurted out their news he leapt to his feet, as if he had two good legs. Lee Sing took a milder interest in the newly discovered gold.

"That is what caused men to do all sorts of terrible things," was all she said when she saw it.

After the excited talk had died down, Bassett looked off toward the river bottom in the darkness. "You know our job is only half done. Yen Ching and his other hatchet man are out there some-where."

"We've got the gold. Why don't we just forget them? After all, what can two men do?"

"Yen Ching is the leader of the most powerful tong in Chinatown," Fred Casey said, spreading out his blanket under the wagon. "You might call him the King of the Highbinders. If he gets away we'll never get the information about who was in on that robbery, in-cluding the insider at the Mint."

"Well, at least this will make him lose face with all the other Chinese who might have been inclined to join this revolution of his," Jay said. "But with the pride and arrogance that man has he'll never stop or give up until he's dead or captured."

"I have a hunch they're down there along the river somewhere," Fred said. "They probably know by now that their hatchet man didn't make it. But they can't know we've found the gold. Even though all the tracks have been scoured out by that storm, I really feel they're not far away, waiting to finish this one way or another."

CHAPTER 18

The sun was just making its appearance
in a cloudless sky over the low desert
mountains the next morning as the four
were finishing breakfast. Breakfast was
the same as supper — bacon and corn
cakes. They stood around the fire, eating
with their fingers since there were no
plates or utensils. Meager fare, Jay reflected. But if they were all as nervous
as he was they were hardly aware of
what they were eating, or if they were
eating at all.

If Fred was right, they were coming to
the end of a long chase. If, indeed, Yen
Ching and his hatchet man were
camped somewhere in the cover along
that river, they would have to flush them
out. Jay didn't like the look of it. He
would much rather have been on the
defensive in such a wooded terrain.
True, the trees, with the exception of a
few giant cottonwoods that had survived

years of floods, were not tall, but they looked to be fairly thick. And there was undergrowth, besides, where a man could hide.

They took their time about finishing breakfast. They wanted the sun well up and throwing as much light as possible before they started. They cleaned up, smothered the fire, put away the corn-meal and bacon, and then cleaned their weapons as best they could of the grit from the dust and sandstorm. They gave Lee Sing the .45 Colt they had taken off the dead highbinder. Since she had no way to carry it, Bassett slipped off his belt and she tried putting it around her. But it was far too big. Not one of them had a belt she could wear, and there were no pockets in the cotton shift she still wore. So she put the gun into the wagon until she might have need of it.

Only when the sun was an hour up did they hitch up the mules and climb into the wagon. Jay took the reins, with Lee Sing beside him and the Secret Service agent and the policeman on the rear seat. Jay wheeled the team around, slapped the reins over their backs, and called to them loudly. They broke into a trot, hauling the wagon back along the road they had come from Ehrenberg. For the benefit of anyone watching from the tree line Jay drove almost a mile, until the road curved and dipped away from the sight of the river. Then he pulled the team to a halt and rested them for a few minutes.

Then, by a prearranged plan, he handed the reins over to Lee Sing and climbed down, along with the other two.

"Stay here and guard the wagon. If you hear any shooting, drive the wagon straight back to Ehrenberg and get help. Ask for the soldier who lives at the Government House. There's a lieutenant on detached duty there who oversees government supplies coming upriver through the warehouse. If he doesn't believe you, show him some of the gold. Your loaded gun is here on the floor beside you but you shouldn't need it. All right?"

She nodded, her face expressionless.

As a precaution, Jay took off his hat and filled it with the last of the water from his large canteen and let the mules drink it all. "You're thirstier than I am, but this'll have to hold you," he muttered, shaking out his hat and replacing it on his head.

Then he joined the others, and they trudged over the rise in the soft sand and out of sight without looking back. They were able to gain the river with very little chance of being seen by anyone who might have been in the woods near La Paz. There was a slight morning breeze as the earth began to warm up again, but the breeze did not penetrate the growth by the river. They stayed just inside the tree line where the growth was thinnest and worked their way northward back toward La Paz.

When they reached the former lagoon that was silted in and studded with growth, they spread out so they were about thirty yards apart and moved more cautiously. They had seen nothing and heard nothing. Thirty minutes passed as they moved another half-mile northward, following the slight curve of the Colorado. Except for a few birds they saw no sign of animate life — until Jay, who was in the lead, startled a mule deer that went bounding away, almost causing Jay to drop his gun in fright. He turned to say something to Fred when a gun roared a few yards away and he felt his left heel go numb. He dropped to the ground instinctively and squeezed off a shot in the general direction of the blast, but he saw no one. Another shot came almost immediately, and then another. Jay could hear Fred returning fire somewhere to his left. Three more shots came, and Jay hugged the ground as he heard one of the slugs rip through the bushes just above his head. Then Jay heard a strangled cry, cut off almost immediately. Then silence for a minute or two that seemed like hours.

"Fred? You okay?" he called out cautiously.

"Yeah. I'm still here. You hit?"

"Not sure. Maybe my left heel."

"Where's Bassett?"

A strange, high-pitched voice cut in. "Your friend is with us, gentlemen. If you will be so kind as to throw your weapons out and step out here, you can see him again."

The sound sent a chill up Jay's sweating back. The last time he had heard that voice he was standing before a throne in the depths of Chinatown. It was Yen Ching!

"Quickly, gentlemen, or your friend's head will be severed from his body."

The urgency in the lunatic voice caused Jay to reply immediately. "All right, all right. We're coming out." He let down the hammer on his Lightning and tossed it high over the weeds a few feet away, making sure it landed in some soft dirt.

He heard a thump a few seconds later as Fred did the same. He raised his hands over his head and stood up, feeling the numb left heel now beginning to pain him as he put weight on it.

"This way, gentlemen," the high-pitched, disembodied voice said.

Jay walked toward the voice, out of the chest-high bushes into the trees. His steps were uneven, and he glanced down at the painful heel. The bullet had torn off the flat boot heel but had only bruised his foot. He expected any second to feel a bullet in his chest. He saw Fred moving toward him at an angle. When they had gone about fifty feet the dreaded Buddha-like figure emerged from behind the trunk of a large cotton-wood. He was holding an Army-model Colt .45 single-action in his pudgy fist. The hole in the seven-and-a-half-inch barrel looked as big as a cannon mouth to Jay as he approached it.

Jay decided to try a little bravado. "Where are your two hatchet men?"

"One of them, as you well know, is dead or disabled. The other is pointing a gun at you this very minute."

Without moving his head Jay flicked his eyes back and forth, but saw nothing of the other man.

"He is holding your man with the wound in his leg," Yen Ching went on. "If either of you two makes any sudden moves, your friend dies."

Yen Ching was never one to waste words unless he was ranting about over-throwing the Manchu rulers.

"What now?" Jay asked, stopping about ten feet from the rotund figure. Even here, along this muddy riverbank, the tong leader was dressed in green brocaded silk, the jacket open down the front, revealing his massive chest and belly. Now he wore a straight-brim black hat on his shaved head. Even though there was still a damp coolness under the trees the fat one was sweating pro-fusley, staining the silk a darker green in several places.

"What now, you ask," the figure re-peated. "I will tell you, Mr. McGraw. You have put me to a considerable inconvenience and, if I were a vengeful man, I could put you to a great deal of pain. However, because I haven't the time nor the inclination to deal with you as you deserve, I will make your end a quick and relatively painless one."

Jay's stomach tensed into a knot at the sound of this. He shot a quick glance at Fred. He was impassive, but Jay thought he looked a little paler than usual.

"This way." Yen Ching waved the gun barrel, and Jay and Fred walked past him. "Straight ahead," he instructed them as they went toward the river. Forty yards farther on they came in sight of the muddy Colorado, roiling along under the morning sun.

"That's far enough."

The pair halted. They stood in a small open space in the trees where a low cooking fire had been hastily put out. The two freight wagons were parked nearby. The mules were nowhere to be seen. Blankets and camp gear were scattered about.

Only then did the other hatchet man appear, half dragging Glen Bassett, his arm crooked about his throat, and holding a knife in the other hand. Bassett's hair was disheveled and his eyes were wide with fear.

"We will not prolong this. There is a shovel by the fire there. Take it."

He held the gun steady, his black, pig-like eyes peering out of the folds of fat.

"Choose a spot and start digging," the fat man ordered.

"Digging for what?"

"For your graves, Mr. Jay McGraw. You don't think I want to throw you in the river and have your bodies turn up somewhere downstream? That might prove . . . uh . . . inconvenient for me. No, this way is much safer and neater, and I've done all the digging I care to do for a while."

With a sinking feeling in the pit of his stomach Jay picked up the shovel and sank the point of it in the earth where he was standing. He worked slowly, stalling for time. He had to figure some way out of this, but it seemed hopeless. If he made a move to escape Bassett would be killed, or he himself shot by Yen Ching, who still held the .45 rock-steady, even though the big man was now leaning back against a tree.

"Come now, Mr. McGraw, I know you

can work faster than that. The quicker you finish the job, the quicker you three will be in paradise. A heavenly paradise — isn't that what you Christians believe in?" He managed a slight smile at his own humor. "Why do you hesitate? Heaven is what you live for your entire life, is it not? I sense a reluctance to leave this earthly suffering for endless joy." His laugh came out as a single bark.

Jay wanted to fling the shovel in his face, but knew it would mean instant death for himself and his companions, so he kept his head down and turned over shovelfuls of dirt. Ten minutes passed, then twenty.

"You there, get over and help him," Yen Ching ordered Fred Casey. "There is another shovel in the nearest wagon."

Bassett was struggling feebly in the grip of the highbinder, so Ah Kow kicked him viciously in his wounded leg and the agent collapsed on the ground, moaning and holding his bandaged leg.

Jay had just lifted his head to watch Fred step up onto the wagon wheel when he saw a flash out of the greenery and a roar shattered the stillness. Yen Ching and his guard both spun toward the noise and fired at the puff of smoke. Jay leapt across the fire and brought the shovel down hard on the fat man's gun arm as he was cocking his Colt again. The gun exploded into the dirt as it flew from his hand.

Bassett, who was still on the ground, tackled the hatchet man's legs from behind. Ah Kow went down. But he twisted around like a cat and fired at Casey, who was coming to help. Because of his awkward position the shot went high, and Fred dove to one side and rolled out of the way before he could fire again. Ah Kow brought the butt of his revolver down hard on Bassett's head and the agent went limp. The hatchet man kicked free and sprang to his feet just as Jay retrieved Yen Ching's Colt. He fired wildly at Jay, who hit the ground beside Fred and cocked the Army Colt. The hammer fell on a spent chamber. The gun was empty.

Yen Ching was staggering around, trying to pick up the shovel, but he was too fat to bend over. Ah Kow, seeing both his foes unarmed, raised his pistol and took deliberate aim.

Just then Lee Sing came bounding out of the woods, holding the big revolver in both hands, and let go with another shot from about ten feet away. The slug shattered Ah Kow's right arm and his shot went wild as the gun fell from his grasp. He staggered sideways with the shock of the bullet but caught his balance and made a weaving rush for the river and plunged in. He came up a few feet from shore, trying valiantly to sidestroke across with his good left arm. But he was caught in a whirlpool and spun crazily around. For a second they saw his face, and then his queue floating out in back of his head, then his face again. He finally broke free of the whirlpool and struck out again. But the main current caught and swept him downstream. A dead snag struck up from the surface like a beckoning finger. Ah Kow reached for it but missed as the water swept him past. He was splashing now, growing noticeably weaker. He must have been losing a lot of blood, and the quilted clothing was water-soaked. They watched, fascinated, as Ah Kow thrashed the water feebly with his good arm. Then he quit thrashing. His head bobbed up and down once, twice, and then he was gone, swallowed up by the muddy red water of the Colorado.

Those on shore stared at the spot where he had gone down. Finally Jay broke the silence. " 'What disappears beneath the Colorado is never seen again,' " he quoted Captain Jack Mellon.

"So it should always be to any warrior of the Chee Kong tong who deserts his master," Yen Ching said. Then he looked at Lee Sing. He said something to her in Chinese, and her face grew slightly flushed and her jaw muscles twitched under the smooth skin. But she never changed expression as she glanced at Jay, as if afraid he might have understood.

While Lee Sing held her gun on Yen Ching, Jay helped a woozy Glen Bassett to his feet. Blood trickled down his forehead from the blow of the gun butt.

Fred climbed into the nearest freight wagon and ripped the lids off a few of the crates to examine their contents.

"Well?" Jay asked as Fred climbed down a few minutes later.

"Just what the label says: a few odds and ends of mining tools — single and double jacks, sledgehammers, crowbars, shovels, cable, some pieces of a windlass, some empty pipe — in fact, just enough stuff to make a good cover for what was really in there."

"What do you intend to do with me now?" Yen Ching asked. "You have just caused yourselves a great deal of trouble. You have stalked, attacked, and killed two simple Chinese merchants trying to go about their business of selling mining machinery."

Fred Casey grinned. "So that's to be the way of it?"

"We fought only to defend ourselves and our property," Yen Ching continued.

"He steals a good chunk of the U.S. Treasury and then wants to hide behind the Constitution," Bassett said, holding both hands to his temples.

"You have no proof that I stole anything. You must have evidence in your courts. You see, I not only know your language and your customs but I also know your law."

"We found the gold buried in the iron pipes right up the hill in La Paz," Jay said. "That should be proof enough."

Yen Ching looked at him somberly. "What has that to do with me? I know of no such gold."

"I'm afraid we have an eyewitness in the form of Lee Sing, who will testify differently, as will Jay McGraw. I believe there is an assayer at the Mint who will also see things differently once he is charged."

"Nothing you can say or do will hurt me or change the outcome of what is to be. I have been destined to become the next emperor of my homeland. It has been revealed to me that I will found a dynasty that will overthrow the Manchus and rule for many generations to come."

As they talked, they were leading Yen Ching through the trees and back toward the slope that led up to the abandoned road. Jay was helping Bassett limp along on his injured leg, while he himself was favoring his bruised left heel.

Yen Ching refused to let them examine the forearm that had been hit with the shovel, so they assumed it was not broken.

"Lee Sing, you are a wonder," Jay said to her as they reached the top of the sandy rise and found the wagon and mules waiting. "You have saved me twice from this crazy man. You saved us all. If you had not used your own judgment and disobeyed my instructions, the only thing the men of Ehrenberg would have found would have been some fresh graves on a muddy river bank. What can we do to thank you?"

"You need to say nothing further, Jay McGraw. If you had not saved me from starving on that island, I would not be here."

They helped Yen Ching into the back-seat of the wagon, which settled down noticeably on its springs under his weight. The rest of them climbed aboard and Jay took the reins. He glanced at the sky and at the face of the beautiful Chinese girl beside him. It was going to be a beautiful day.

CHAPTER 19

"What will happen to Yen Ching if he's convicted?" Jay asked three weeks later as he, Fred Casey, and Lee Sing sat sipping hot tea following a meal in one of Chinatown's best restaurants.

Fred shook his head. "He may go to prison for life. But since he's not a citizen of this country, he might be deported to China."

"Then he'll just be on the loose again," Jay said.

"After all the testimony that has come out at his trial, including what you gave, I think not."

"Why's that?"

"The Manchu rulers don't take kindly to revolutionaries. If he's sent back to China he'll be beheaded. Those Manchu dictators have no sense of humor. They'll lop off a head at the drop of a hat, so to speak. Some of the lesser criminals who've been deported from Chinatown have lost their heads.

"I think once he's out of the way there won't be any trouble with the rest of the Chee Kong tong members, even though only a few of them were arrested and charged. It's like whacking off the head of a snake."

"So it was the assayer at the Mint who was the inside man on the robbery?"

"Yes. He was the one who fed the information about the time, place, and route of the delivery from the Mint to the depot. With that, Yen Ching was able to make all his plans."

"Too bad they found only half the gold," Jay said, sipping at the lukewarm tea.

Casey nodded. "My estimate of the weight was off. The weight of three million in double eagles was excessive so they decided to split it up and not put all their eggs in one basket. From all that Yen Ching has said — and he couldn't resist doing a little bragging — the other half of that gold is probably in China now with some of his revolutionary sympathizers. I doubt the government will ever recover it, even if the Manchu government somehow gets their hands on it."

"Well, the fact that they had only half the gold on the train explains why they didn't have all three hundred or so of those coffins we saw them load onto the ship. They shipped about a hundred and fifty crates to Yuma on those two extra freight cars that were uncoupled there and they loaded all hundred and fifty onto the *Mohave II* for the trip up-river, but there was gold in only about a third of them. The rest of the crates that didn't contain a special marking were left on the boat to go on to Fort Mojave where they were unloaded and left. It was just another ploy to throw us off the track. The fifty crates containing the gold were unloaded at Ehrenberg when Yen Ching and his two hatchet men got off. They rented the wagons to haul the approximately two tons of gold. Each crate weighed about two hundred pounds, counting the gold and the few tools packed in with the loaded pipes to make it look legitimate in case someone should open them."

"But why were they going upstream?" Jay asked.

"Yen Ching hasn't even admitted to stealing it yet, but the big chiefs at the department think they were trying to stash it somewhere safe until things cooled off and then retrieve it later and take it to Mexico. They knew the border was being watched, along with Port Ysabel at the mouth of the Colorado. The Secret Service had also alerted the Mexican government to search any ship arriving in Mexican ports from the United States. That's probably why they unloaded at Los Angeles and hauled it overland. They would have passed for just what they pretended to — innocent Chinese merchants — had it not been for us recognizing the name of the *City of Peking* as the same ship that had loaded those coffins here a few days before it turned up in Los Angeles."

"If my beer wagon contained only half the gold, how did they get the other half safely hidden and then out of the country?" Jay wanted to know.

Fred shook his head. "Nobody knows that for sure yet. It may yet come out at the trial. I hear the lawyers have offered to push for a lighter sentence for the assayer if he will give testimony against the tong and provide them with details. It'll make fascinating reading. The *Police Gazette* has already jumped on it, and this trial is making newspaper headlines around the country. You and I are heroes." Fred grinned and toasted him with a small glass of rice wine.

"Here's to our new status," Jay grinned back, raising his glass. He took a tiny sip. He hated the taste of rice wine since Lee Sing had drugged him with it the first time he had seen her.

"They're still investigating to see if someone at Wieland's Brewery was in on it, but they haven't been able to break the old German — Carl Bauer's — story, and they have no proof so far. I guess the reason the tong selected the brewery to stash the gold is that it's on Second Street and the Mint's on Fifth — not far apart," Fred said.

"What still bothers me is why a leader like Yen Ching would have taken the risk to accompany that gold himself, instead of ordering his subordinates to haul it inland and hide it."

"I don't know," Fred replied. "Yen Ching loved luxury and ease and plea-sure, but he had a hard core and wanted to be close to the action. We found out he had been a warrior in his youth. One of his weaknesses was that he could not trust his men to handle all that gold without being there himself to direct their every move, even though it was physically hard on him."

"Too bad about Glen Bassett," Jay remarked, changing the subject.

"Sure was. His bosses accepted all the public praise for his part in the capture of Yen Ching and the gold. Then they demoted him and transferred him to Washington, D.C., for letting Yen Ching get away from Los Angeles and then for failing to properly notify his superiors while we were on the trail."

"How was he supposed to do that?"

"They said he could have telegraphed San Francisco or Washington from Tucson."

"Even if he had, the Secret Service couldn't have gotten men there any quicker than we got there," Jay said.

Fred shrugged. "I know. But the chiefs are puffed up with self-importance and take themselves very seriously. It's a price you pay for working for Uncle Sam. Last time I saw him Glen said he was in a big argument with the finance people of his service over his travel expenses. He didn't get receipts for some of the things he bought and claimed for reimbursement — like the shirt we tore up to bandage his leg."

"You're joking!" Jay was aghast.

"I'm afraid not. He helped capture one of the most notorious criminals in the country and recovered about a million and a half in gold, and they won't pay him for a two-dollar shirt."

Jay shook his head in disbelief. "The man deserves better than that."

"What are you going to do with your reward money from Wells Fargo? You know they would have gone bankrupt if they had been forced to make good on that loss."

"Well, the frrst thing I'm going to do is invest your share of it in something so that it'll make you some money if you ever decide to quit the police force and are allowed to accept a reward."

"It's amazing how many people think I already take bribes and payoffs as a member of the special police squad in Chinatown, as some of the other policemen do."

"Did I tell you that when I turned in my temporary detective's badge to your captain the other day, I was called down to the Wells Fargo office and offered a job?"

"No."

"They said they were impressed with

my resourcefulness and they were looking for good young men to bring into the company."

"What would you be doing? Working in their office or bank?"

"No. They want to start me as a shotgun messenger guarding express cars on cross-country trains."

"Sounds better than driving a beer wagon."

"Do you think I should take it, Lee Sing?" he asked, turning to the girl who had sat silent during most of the conversation. She was dressed in white silk trimmed with a border of tiny blue flowers. Her black hair shone in the candlelight from the center of their table.

"You can do anything you wish, Jay McGraw," she replied in that musical voice, looking at him with her soft brown eyes. "I'm sure you will do well at it."

"Is your mind set on returning to China when the trial ends?"

"Yes. With the money from the reward, I will be able to help my family very much. I'm sure they have heard by now that I was captured and brought here as a slave to Yen Ching. They did not know what happened to me when I disappeared. Now it will be a joyous home-coming for all of us."

"Will I ever see you again?" he asked hesitantly.

She smiled at him. "Of course. I will return to this country, at least to visit." She reached across and touched his cheek lightly. "How could I leave a good friend and never return?"

Casey looked at the two of them. "Before this gets too serious, I think we should all adjourn to Boyle's Saloon for a mug of steam beer and maybe a song or two to cap off this evening."

Jay thought there had never been a better time to be alive, and living in the Big City by the Golden Hills.

Tim Champlin, born John Michael Champlin in Fargo, North Dakota, was graduated from Middle Tennessee State University and earned a Master's degree from Peabody College in Nashville, Tennessee. Beginning his career as an author of the Western story with SUMMER OF THE SIOUX in 1982, the American West represents for him "a huge, ever-changing block of space and time in which an individual had more freedom than the average person has today. . . . For those brave, and sometimes desperate souls who ventured West looking for a better life, it must have been an exciting time to be alive." Champlin has achieved a notable stature in being able to capture that time in complex, often exciting, and historically accurate fictional narratives. Currently at work on his first non-series Western novel, his previous work has been concerned with two series characters, Matt Tierney, who comes of age in SUMMER OF THE SIOUX and who begins his professional career as a reporter for the Chicago *Times-Herald* covering an expeditionary force venturing into the Big Horn country and the Yellowstone, and Jay McGraw, a callow youth who is plunged into outlawry at the beginning of COLT LIGHTNING. There are six books in the Matt Tierney series and five featuring Jay McGraw. However, in all of Champlin's stories, there are always unconventional plot ingredients, striking historical details, vivid characterizations of the multitude of ethnic and cultural diversity found on the frontier, and narratives rich and original and surprising. His exuberant tapestries include lumber schooners sailing the West Coast, early-day wet-plate photography, daredevils who thrill crowds with gas balloons and the first parachutes, Tong Wars in San Francisco's Chinatown, Basque sheepherders, and the Penitentes of the Southwest, and are always highly entertaining.

We hope you have enjoyed this Large Print book. Other Thorndike Press or Chivers Press Large Print books are available at your library or directly from the publishers.

For more information about current and upcoming titles, please call or write, without obligation, to:

Thorndike Press
P.O. Box 159
Thorndike, Maine 04986 USA
Tel. (800) 223-2336

OR

Chivers Press Limited
Windsor Bridge Road
Bath BA2 3AX
England
Tel. (0225) 335336

All our Large Print titles are designed for easy reading, and all our books are made to last.